Possibly Dangerous

Short Fiction

Alby Stone

A Bad Apple (30 June 2013), *Before Tomorrow* (28 March 2013), *Flowers in the Rain* (17 August 2014), *My Torture Porn Hell* (28 March 2015), *Nature in the Raw* (23 July 2013), *Nobody Special* (22 December 2015), *Pyromancer* (7 May 2015), *Suspicious Minds* (11 November 2014), and *Tinsel* (7 December 2014) were all previously published on the Vainglorious Lunacy website. http://vaingloriouslunacy.com

Bullshit Detector (12 November 2014) and *Haunted House* (2 October 2014) were previously published on the Clerkenwell Writers Asylum website. http://clerkenwellwritersasylum.wordpress.com/

Boracic Park, Hot Love, Imago, Fatal Attractor, Laurel Beach, The Minder, The Netherwold Heritage, Pop! and *Significant, Other* are published here for the first time.

The cover illustration was created from a photograph taken by the author and manipulated using PaintShop® Pro and the online Deep Dream Generator (http://www.deepdreamgenerator.com).

Copyright © 2016 Alby Stone

All rights reserved.

ISBN-10: 1539159108
ISBN-13: 978-1539159100

Contents

Introduction i
Significant, Other 1
Pop! 23
Hot Love 30
A Bad Apple 42
Bullshit Detector 50
Tinsel 59
Fatal Attractor 72
Nobody Special 90
Laurel Beach 104
The Minder 114
Nature in the Raw 137
My Torture Porn Hell 147
Flowers in the Rain 168
Suspicious Minds 172
Boracic Park 180
Before Tomorrow 190
Pyromancer 198
Imago 203
Haunted House 209
The Netherwold Heritage 212
About the Author

Introduction

The stories in this book – a varied assemblage of diversions, entertainments and experiments – were written between January 2013 and September 2016. Eleven have previously appeared on the Vainglorious Lunacy or Clerkenwell Writers Asylum websites, and have been corrected or lightly revised for this collection. Nine stories are published here for the first time.

Alby Stone
Walworth, London
September 2016

Significant, Other

A pillow, damp with sweat; weak sunlight sneaking through a gap in the blinds. A faint smell of petrol and singed hair. That's what Miranda Hawkes wakes up to this morning. The duvet is off the bed, her feet are tangled in the bottom sheet, and one arm is still asleep where she's been lying on it. Her long auburn tresses have spontaneously twisted into surrealistic dreadlocks. Her face is smeared randomly with substances that were once carefully-applied cosmetics. The bathroom mirror isn't kind at the best of times but today she could pass for an extra from *The Evil Dead* – the one in the scene they didn't use because it was too frightening.

She refuses to look in the toilet bowl before flushing. In the shower her wet, unusually tender skin sticks to the plastic curtain, and for no reason she flinches, thinks of Laura Palmer, Janet Leigh. Brushing her teeth makes her appear vaguely rabid. She tries not to think about the way she looks. She tries not to think about anything.

Breakfast progresses in eerie normality. For once there is no stack of greasy dishes and cutlery in the sink, so she can get stuck into slicing bread, opening cartons and putting the kettle on without having to work for it. The toast and orange juice are consumed, even enjoyed. She doesn't mind the crumbs flecking her dressing gown or the careless dribbles of liquid sweetening the corners of her mouth. But over the coffee, Miranda cracks. She thinks of last night. Had it really happened the way she remembered? Had it even happened at all?

Well, yes. It had really happened – a night more wild and extraordinary than anything she'd ever imagined. A night that left her exhausted and aching, bruised and sore, scorched in intimate places. A night of terror, wonder and horror. A night when she'd done unspeakable, indescribable things. It had been too much to bear. It had also been exhilarating and liberating, and unbelievably pleasurable. She'd loved every second of it.

Thirty-seven years old, childless, acrimoniously divorced and now socially isolated, Miranda didn't see herself as the poster girl for post-modern feminism. True, she had a decent job as a financial advisor, a job in which she had once been both respected – in professional terms if nothing else – and successful, the only woman in a key team, one of the elite. It was also a fact that, on a good day, she was physically attractive; although she did, she admitted, usually look either severe or dispirited, depending on how her life outside work was going. It was also true that she had struck what she considered a mighty blow for women everywhere by getting shot of that feckless, unfaithful, conceited and mouthy oaf Jack Chappell, whose wife she was until not so long ago. Now there was a waste of a perfectly good walk down a church aisle and a few square yards of dishonestly-virginal white lace. She'd managed to keep the flat but at least she didn't have to keep the arsehole's surname.

Some women would have said they were, for the most part, feminist acts. But Miranda didn't see it that way. In her own eyes, she was a victim. The bastard had done his best to blacken her name in any way he could. In court, she was an overbearing, unreasonable, demanding shrew, a sexually insatiable woman who made passes at anyone who took her fancy, male and female alike. The character assassination escalated, illustrated with imaginary memories and fake anecdotes. On Facebook and Twitter, she was a slut, a whore, a gold-digger, a termagant, a lesbian – anything he hated in a woman. Except for the first two, obviously. The man had happily unzipped for plenty of those while she was at home keeping the marital bed warm for his return. His response to her finally having had enough of his despicable behaviour wasn't a surprise. But other people's reactions had been a huge shock. Her family and friends had actually believed the lies. Invitations and phone calls dried up, she found herself an outcast on social media, and her suggestions for weekend drinks and outings went unanswered.

Inevitably, Miranda's colleagues got wind of it. The women looked down their noses. Some of the braver men brazenly propositioned her. The canteen and water-cooler, once the places she went to for gossip and a laugh, became the source of sniggers and sideways glances, knowing grins and frowns of disapproval. The high-profile tasks and opportunities for advancement came to an abrupt end. How could her employers place their faith a woman who'd turned on her own husband, a saintly man whose only sin was to try in vain to please his appalling bitch of a wife?

How could her female co-workers trust a woman like that with their husbands and boyfriends? How could the men she worked with trust her with their wives and girlfriends? Soon enough, Miranda had been downgraded. Once the company's golden girl, she was now seen only as a tarnished brass.

Then, just as she was beginning to think she might as well flush her life down the toilet and get herself to a nunnery – then, there was Paris.

It was a sudden whim. One November day she got it into her head that she needed a break, a change of scene. Maybe it was also time to realise an old ambition. Miranda had never been to Paris. The city had been her original choice for a honeymoon, but her ex-millstone and tormentor from beyond the Decree Absolute had sulked and skulked until he got his way and they'd ended up in bloody Corfu, where she was bored rigid and he was no doubt fantasising about being rigid and boring his way through all those bikini-clad bodies on the beach. Paris next year, he promised. The promise was repeated every year until she found out what he'd really been up to on all those business trips.

An hour online and the arrangements were complete. Eurostar tickets, a week in a hotel not far from the Gare du Nord, with a night out at the Moulin Rouge and a carnet of Metro tickets thrown in. Her local bookshop provided the *Rough Guide* to Paris and, at the recommendation of the girl at the till, *The Da Vinci Code*, which she donated to the nearest charity shop after only fifty-three pages. She didn't buy anything special to wear. It was to be a holiday, not a fashion shoot. And besides, she'd pretty much run out of expectations. All she wanted was a week with nothing to weigh her down, a few days of Montmartre and Notre Dame, the Louvre and the Seine, patisseries and wine – *Paris*.

And it was wonderful. She could barely speak the language, got lost on the Metro, miscounted her euros in restaurants, ate food she was sure she hadn't ordered – and loved every minute of it. In Paris she was anonymous. Parisians were rude to everyone, so she fitted in nicely. Sometimes they seemed to know instinctively that she was English, but mostly when they spoke first it was in French, which pleased her immensely. It made her feel as if she belonged. For the first time since the divorce, Miranda was alone without feeling lonely. After three days she began to seriously consider selling up, jacking in her job and moving to the City of Lights.

On the fourth day she went for a walk, getting lost again but fortuitously finding herself crossing the Pont Neuf to the Île de la Cité. Up to then she'd only been there to look at the cathedral, Notre Dame de Paris, but the island was a location she was determined to explore. This time she wandered the length of the island, aware of its long history, from the ancient Gauls, who built the temple on which the cathedral now stood; to Marie Antoinette, languishing in the Conciergerie before her appointment with Madame Guillotine. The island had housed kings and saints; by the Pont Neuf the Knights Templar leader Jacques de Molay had been burned at the stake. Prisons and palaces and places of worship of all ages clustered there at the heart of Paris. In some ways it reminded Miranda of the older parts of London; in other ways it was very different.

But it was the modern Mémorial des Martyrs de la Déportation that threw her world wholly out of kilter.

The architecture was brutal and claustrophobic, a narrow crypt beneath ugly concrete blocks. But when she descended into the cramped space, before her eyes adjusted to the changed light, she had a fleeting sense of wonder. The walls seemed to be studded with thousands of fireflies. On closer inspection, they turned out to be small pieces of glass or crystal illuminated by an unseen source of light. And there were inscriptions. Miranda strove to decipher them as she wandered through the crypt and into the rotunda.

'*I have dreamt so very much of you,*

I have walked so much,

Loved your shadow so much,

That nothing more is left to me of you.

All that remains to me is to be the shadow among shadows

To be a hundred times more of a shadow than the shadow

To be the shadow that will come and come again into your sunny life.'

She started at the man's sudden, unexpected appearance, the quiet but resonant voice. She'd thought she was alone down there. 'I'm sorry?'

He laughed softly, sadly. He was tall, thin and pale, a little older than her, dark hair and eyes, a black suit and tie, a slight Irish accent. 'The inscription you were looking at. It's a poem by Robert Desnos. He was a surrealist poet who was a member of the Resistance. He died of typhus in the political section of the Terezin concentration camp in June 1945 – after it had been liberated. A cruel irony, though I doubt that he saw the funny side. The other texts are by

Louis Aragon, Paul Éluard, Antoine de Saint-Exupéry, Jean-Paul Sartre.'

'Oh. Thank you. How did you know I was English?'

He shrugged, a perfunctory gesture that could as easily have been a shiver. 'I didn't, but I guessed you were an Anglophone. You're carrying the *Rough Guide* – in English. It wasn't exactly a stretch. On holiday?'

Miranda nodded, trying to look less flustered than she felt. 'Only for a week. I've always wanted to come to Paris.'

'Do you like it?'

She smiled. 'I think it's wonderful. I'm not so sure about this place, though. It's a bit…' She gazed around the crypt, lost for words.

'It's gloomy, depressing? Holocaust memorials are always that, and usually monolithic in some way, though always impressive. Have you seen the one in Berlin? No? Well, make sure to see it if you go to Germany. There's more to this one than meets the eye, mind you. That bright light at the end of the tunnel is a bit obvious, but there are some more subtle touches. The inscription on that round plaque set in the floor – *They descended into the mouth of the earth and they did not return*. And over the exit – *Forgive but never forget*. Yet we do forget, don't we? Xenophobia and racial hatred are worse now than at any time since the Nazis were defeated. And politicians are the worst, always eager to pander to the electorate's basest instincts just to get a few more crosses on ballot papers.'

The bitterness in his voice was unmistakeable. She took a step back, alarmed by his intensity. 'I'm sorry, I'm not really interested in politics.'

'No, I'm the one who should be sorry,' he smiled

wryly. 'Please forgive my preaching. I forget that most people don't share my passion, at least not to the same degree.'

Miranda was intrigued. The question was out before she realised it might lead to a dangerous reply. 'And what is your passion?' *Oh shit, did I really say that? What if he thinks I'm making a pass at him?*

'Justice,' he said. 'And justice dictates that I must buy you a coffee to make up for disturbing you.'

'What part of Ireland are you from?'

'Oh, here and there. I'm not actually Irish, mind, though I did spend a long time there before I moved to the Continent a few years back. It's a long story, mostly too dull to bear thinking about.'

They were sitting at tables on the pavement, despite the grey sky and gathering clouds outside. He looked up at the sky, pursed his lips. 'It's going to rain in a bit.' He fished a pack of Gauloise and a cheap Bic lighter from his jacket pocket, lit a cigarette, inhaled, coughed, inhaled again. 'So tell me about yourself, Miranda.'

To her surprise, she did just that, marvelling at how easy it was to talk to this stranger who, to tell the truth, was actually a little bit frightening.

'If you don't mind me saying,' he observed when she'd given him the abridged version of her autobiography, 'your ex sounds like a bit of a shit. But he's not atypical, Miranda. Another depressing symptom of the time. The more legal equality women get, the more they prove they're as good as men, the more some men hate them.'

'What about you? You haven't even told me your

name or what you do for a living.'

'Ah, so the coffee isn't enough for you – you want more out of me. OK, my name's Malachi McSheed. I'm a consultant, a facilitator.'

'I thought you said you're not Irish? And what do you consult and facilitate about?'

He grinned. He wasn't bad looking, though Miranda kept revising her estimate of his age up and down. *It's those eyes*, she thought, *such a dark brown they seem almost black. Sometimes they crinkle with humour and he looks like a very young man; but when he gets serious they're an old man's eyes.*

'I can be Irish when it suits me. I suppose technically I was born an Israeli. Or a Palestinian. Take your pick. My father could never make up his bloody mind on that particular subject. We don't really get on – he's very religious, I'm not. I left the so-called Holy Land a very long time ago. Been around the block a few times, as they say. As for my work – I find solutions to difficult problems.'

'What sort of problems?'

The old man's eyes returned. 'Like I said, I have a passion for justice. I advise communities and individuals that have been victims of hate crime. It's a free service; my vocation, you might say. If I am offered payment it goes to charities that help victims of injustice. I don't need money.'

'I'm not sure what you mean by "hate crime",' said Miranda. 'Do you mean racist attacks, queer-bashing, people burning down mosques and synagogues, that sort of thing?'

Malachi frowned, though his eyes twinkled. 'It's a bit broader than that. When something unjust or unfair is done to someone – an individual or a group – simply because the perpetrator hates who or what they are, that's a hate crime. Trolling on Facebook or Twitter are hate crimes. I would argue that all male violence against women is a hate crime. Any bad action carried out because of bigotry or prejudice. So-called ethnic cleansing, homophobia, rape… It's a long list. And it's going to get longer. Look at the growth of the extreme Right in Europe – they even have MEPs, for crying out loud. Fascists and racists pretending to be democrats. The popular newspapers in every European country are baying like hounds about immigrants and Islam; homosexuality is being criminalised again in some places. Even anti-Semitism is on the rise again. That monument we were in just now – I go to places like that every once in a while just to remind myself of how bad it can get, and renew my determination to ensure it doesn't. *Forgive but never forget*. We mustn't even be bigoted against the bigots. That's the really hard part.'

She laughed, even though his rising intensity was again unsettling. *'To err is human, to forgive, divine.'*

Malachi echoed her laughter. 'That's the only Pope I ever had time for.'

When he laughed like that he was mesmerising – just so damned sexy. Miranda took a deep breath. 'If you don't have anything planned for tomorrow, how about showing me some of the more out-of-the-way places? I fancy going a bit off the beaten track.'

After Paris, London seemed grey and two-dimensional. But it wasn't a simple matter of coming home to resume an existent that now seemed both purposeless and commonplace, or that London had in any way become a lesser city. Miranda was honest enough to admit that parts of Paris were as run-down and dull as anywhere in London, while London had its own delights and surprises to match anything the French capital could offer. No, there was a simpler reason for the disaffection, her new alienation. Malachi McSheed was not there.

How had it happened? How on earth had she become so obsessed with this strange man she'd known for less than three days? On her first night back, as she lay in bed waiting in vain for sleep, she tried to talk herself out of it. He smoked. He was changeable, occasionally distant, sometimes a bit too intense, and disinclined to talk about himself. Actually, that last was a good thing in a man, so she added it to the list of his positive traits. He was knowledgeable, intelligent, unfailingly polite, usually calm, and could be very considerate and attentive. She liked the way he always seemed to know what she was thinking and feeling, the way he responded to her moods. He was clearly caring and compassionate. And he smelled very nice, something that reminded her of roses, with a faint suggestion of the sea – though to be fair, that could just have been her hormones playing olfactory tricks.

She sighed into the darkness of her bedroom. The pluses outweighed the minuses, damn it. But why hadn't he made even the slightest attempt to get her into bed? Chivalry was all very well, but in this day and age a woman expected a man to at least suggest that he found her sexually attractive. Christ, she'd practically thrown herself at him that last night and he still hadn't taken the hint. But at least he'd responded to the kiss and, with a trace of fire in his eyes that she could only interpret as a sign of arousal, produced a business card.

'I'll be in London on Tuesday evening,' he said. 'Call me. I'll take you out for dinner. And after…'

And that was it. He left her at the door to her hotel room, trembling with – *yes, admit it* – frustrated lust. There she was, as horny as hell and practically begging for it, and the object of her desire had merely smiled mysteriously and melted into the night. All she had was a business card with a name and a telephone number in gilt lettering. Even the bloody card smelled like him.

What was he exactly? Not really a boyfriend or a lover – not yet, at any rate. Not even a casual shag, worse luck. But there was definitely something between them. They'd bonded. He made her feel like no man ever had before. It wasn't love, either. She hadn't fallen in love with him. Not quite and not yet. That sort of thing takes time, longer than three days in Paris, no matter how good they'd been. No, she had it now – he was her *significant other*. It was a phrase she'd heard but never really understood, not until now, when it finally made sense. Her significant other.

She sat up, switched on the bedside lamp and took the card from the cabinet drawer, closing her eyes and inhaling the scent, picturing his face. God, she wanted him so badly. Before she knew it, her hand was creeping down beneath the duvet, between her legs. She sighed again, first pretending it was his hand, not hers; then that it wasn't his hand at all.

Keith Armitage bore a slight resemblance to the entertainer Michael McIntyre, a likeness he was keen to exploit. He had adopted the same hairstyle, similar mannerisms, and habitually kept up a constant stream of weak puns and bad jokes. He was not a naturally funny man. On this particular Monday morning, even the cheapest gags had deserted him. He was sombre and straight-faced, though Miranda detected something else in his demeanour. He wouldn't meet her eyes. And she was sure he was excited. He got straight down to business. No enquiries as to her health or questions about her holiday. Not even a 'good morning'.

'Do you know why I wanted to see you?'

She shook her head. 'I can't say I do, Keith. I only got into work ten minutes ago. And I was early, as usual. I was making coffee when Nardiya told me you wanted to see me urgently.'

Armitage stood, gazed out of the tenth-floor window at the drab Docklands landscape and muttered something she couldn't make out.

'I'm sorry, I didn't hear that.'

He tutted, turned to face her, still avoiding eye contact. 'I said, there have been allegations. Last week I received an e-mail claiming that you've been siphoning money from clients' accounts. Quite a considerable sum, apparently. There were attachments, scanned copies of bank statements showing regular deposits into your account, in addition to your salary, going back several years. Ten thousand pounds a month. The bank codes match clients in your portfolio.'

'That's impossible,' said Miranda, stunned. 'I've never acted improperly, not once. I haven't even been *tempted*. And I check my statements carefully each month so I know those deposits were never made. Whatever you've been sent, they're forgeries.' She offered him her phone. 'Here, you can call my bank now and clear this up.'

'I'm sorry,' Armitage replied. 'It's out of my hands now. In line with company policy, the police have been notified. Pending the outcome of their investigation, you are suspended without pay. As you know, that too is company policy. A security guard will escort you to your workstation, where you may remove only personal items that have no bearing on your work here. He will then escort you from the premises. You will not be allowed back until such a time as the allegation is disproven. If it transpires that there is a case to answer, criminal proceedings will be initiated. Do you understand?'

Miranda lost her temper. 'Of course I understand, you patronising bastard,' she snapped. 'I'm not a fucking child. But I'm telling you here and now, this is a set-up. I'm good at my job and I've made this firm a lot of money over the years. Not once has any client expressed anything but complete satisfaction with my work. And you know I'm trustworthy, Keith.'

He sneered. 'Trustworthy? Is that what you call yourself? After the way you treated your poor husband? Everyone's talking about your infidelities, the way you flaunt yourself. Nobody here trusts you, Miranda Hawkes. You had them all fooled for a long, long time, but not any more. Hell, you even had me fooled. It's my own fault, I suppose. Too trusting for my own bloody good. I mean, it's obvious now that you're a prize bitch and a bit of a tart, but that's OK as long as you don't have your hand in the till. And let's face it, having a girl around who spreads her legs for all and sundry can be good for morale – it keeps the boys happy and I like a happy team. I'd be prepared to put up with that, but not embezzlement. And for what it's worth, it was a shock. Why, if Jack hadn't –' He shut his mouth abruptly, realising he'd said too much.

'Jack? My ex-husband? *He* sent you that pack of lies? Well, well. And you believe that nasty piece of shit but not me?'

'The evidence is compelling.'

'The evidence is fake. That's what my bank will confirm and what the police will conclude. OK, if this is the way you want to play it, let's play. I'll see you at the tribunal. I mean, there's no way I can work here anymore after what you've just said, is there? Constructive dismissal, sexual harassment, victimisation. This is going to cost the company a pretty penny, Keith. The Board will not be at all pleased with you. Maybe you'd better start thinking about clearing *your* bloody desk.'

Miranda stormed to the door, where a bulky uniformed man was visible through the patterned glass. As she opened the door, she turned.

'And for the record, there's not one man in this firm I'd spread my legs for. None of you are man enough for me.'

She hadn't cried. The anger was too great, that and the desire for revenge overwhelming all other emotions. Surprisingly, she slept well that night, relieved that the misery of work had finally come to a head. Whatever happened now, she was free of the innuendo and no longer had to worry about her colleagues' coolness. She was really looking forward to the tribunal. There would be compensation, a good deal of it. She would have Keith Armitage's shrivelled little testicles as mantelpiece ornaments. Vengeance would be hers, and it would be sweet, so sweet.

At noon the next day, a little apprehensively, she phoned Malachi McSheed. She'd steeled herself for disappointment. The number would be unreachable, perhaps even false. He would still be in Paris, having forgotten all about her. A woman would answer with a voice like winter. The only scenario she wasn't really prepared for was the one she found herself dealing with.

'Hi Miranda,' he said brightly. 'I'm so glad you called. I've booked a table at a nice Italian place in Soho, eight this evening. I did wonder about a French restaurant, but everyone loves Italian food, don't they? I'll text you the name and address. And after we've eaten…' He laughed, a joyous sound that made her weak at the knees. 'I have a surprise for you, something really special. See you later. I can't wait.'

Her side of the conversation hadn't been worth remembering. Tongue-tied and stammering, she was certain Malachi hadn't understood a thing she said. That was fine, though – the important thing, the *only* thing, was that he wanted to see her. He couldn't wait, in fact. Well, she would have a special surprise for him, too. This called for a shopping trip. A new dress, some serious lingerie, something sheer and black – and stockings. Yes, stockings. All men liked them, or so she'd heard. Maybe that was why she'd never worn them for the despicable Jack, though she doubted that would have stopped him taking his sordid pleasures elsewhere.

She dismissed that thought. Jack was history, as ancient as the Merovingian kings who had made Paris their capital city. For an instant she pictured Jack burning at the stake, like Jacques de Molay, screaming in agony as the flames consumed him, hair crisped and withering, flesh charred and bubbling, eyeballs bursting and running from empty sockets. Now that was an immensely satisfying image. What the hell, while she was cleaning out her now-former employers at the tribunal she might as well sue that contemptible bastard for libel. He'd bloody well burn if she had anything to say about it.

He was already seated at a table when she arrived, studying the menu, sipping sparkling mineral water. The wide smile when he looked up and saw her was a very good sign, though not as good as the hug and kiss when he stood to greet her. She had to sit down pretty quickly. There was no denying it, the touch of his lips turned her insides to jelly. She wondered what the touch of other body parts might do to her.

Malachi was evidently in good spirits, happy to see her. It made him seem incredibly young, so much so that he could have been in his early twenties. The other diners probably thought he was her toyboy. Well, they could think whatever they wanted.

The food was excellent and Malachi's conversation was as interesting and enigmatic as it had been in Paris. Miranda drank three glasses of Verdicchio Classico with her lasagne. Malachi, tucking into spaghetti, stuck to water. 'I'm driving,' he explained, with an uncharacteristic wink that set Miranda's heart racing. All through the meal, throughout the conversation, all she could think about was getting Malachi in the sack. Yet that didn't distract her from the food or the wine – indeed, her increasing arousal seemed to enhance flavour and texture. The music – cheesy Italian ballads sung by a Dean Martin wannabe – sounded ethereal and sensual. The waiter's smiles seemed just a little salacious, as if he knew exactly what she was thinking and how she was feeling, and when he offered black pepper he appeared to be perfectly well aware that the large peppermill put her in mind of a giant penis.

As usual, Malachi seemed to read her mind. He grinned wickedly and sucked slowly on a strand of spaghetti, finishing with a languid lick of his lips. Warmth flooded Miranda's groin. *Move over, Mrs Waters.*

Outside, she realised she was slightly drunk. The chilly fresh air cleared her head, but only a little. 'Where are we going now?'

'My car's parked in Soho Square. I'm going to take you for a drive.'

'Where are you staying?'

'I know a place. It's south of the river. Shouldn't take more than forty minutes at this time of night. Here we are.'

He held the door open for her. She liked that. Malachi was such a gentleman. 'What kind of car is this? It looks like a Volkswagen Beetle, but it seems terribly old-fashioned. Actually, it looks a bit – knackered.'

'It is a Volkswagen,' he replied. 'But it's a very early model, a 1937 KdF-Wagen. I restored it myself. KdF stands for *Kraft durch Freude* – strength through joy. I like to maintain a sense of irony in my work. That's why when I'm working I drive a vehicle designed and manufactured by a regime that perpetrated the biggest hate crime in history.'

'It's only a car,' Miranda pointed out.

'No, it's a symbol of what I do and why I do it.'

'Well, I hope you're not working tonight,' said Miranda, alarmed at the prospect of accompanying Malachi on one of his consultations. Working holidays were one thing, but a working *date*? 'I thought we supposed to be having fun. You said you had a special surprise for me.'

Malachi smiled. 'I'm always working, Miranda. I work to stamp out hate. Tell me, what's the opposite of hate?'

'Love,' she sighed contentedly, relieved that the evening seemed to be back on track.

'Then that's what your surprise will be. Your heart's desire. An act of love.'

Miranda grinned inwardly. Now *that* was more like it.

They were somewhere near Barnes Common, she was sure. Precisely where didn't matter, because it wouldn't be long now until she was comparing the reality of Malachi McSheed against her wild fantasies of the last few nights. By the time the car pulled into the tree-lined driveway of a large, unlit house and he killed the engine, Miranda was almost panting.

He climbed out of the car, hurried round to the passenger side and opened the door for her. She slid out of her seat, deliberately revealing a lot of leg, and a glimpse of pale thigh and stocking-top.

'You feel hot,' he said as he took her hand to help her out.

'Oh, I'm hot,' she laughed shakily. 'I'm so hot I can barely believe it. I hope I don't have to wait too much longer for my special surprise.'

'Soon,' he whispered. 'Very soon.'

He led her to a front door, unlocked it, and she followed him inside and along a dark hallway. To one side there was an open door, through which she saw a large and comfortable-looking sofa. Then they passed a staircase and moved into a kitchen. He selected another key and unlocked the back door.

'Where the hell are we going?' she asked. They weren't going upstairs to a bedroom and they weren't even going to have sex on that inviting sofa. What did he have in mind? An energetic romp on the lawn?

'You'll see,' he told her as he opened the door and stepped into a garden.

The garden was quite big, surrounded by high brick walls and with a fringe of willows. In most respects it was an ordinary suburban garden. But what stood in the middle of the lawn was anything but ordinary. A sturdy wooden stake, about six feet high, its base hidden by pieces of wood and bundles of straw. And, chained to the stake, naked, gagged and shivering with cold and fear, a man she knew only too well.

'Jack?' The single word was practically a squeak by the time it left her mouth, though it had started out in her mind as a stream of angry invective. Miranda turned to Malachi. To her astonishment, he looked even younger, like a boy in his late teens. And he was clutching a can. By the time Miranda recovered her wits he had twisted off the cap and was sprinkling liquid over the wood and straw, over Jack. She smelled petrol.

'Malachi? What's *he* doing here?' She sounded like a little girl.

'This is a man who hates,' said Malachi, pointing at the

desperately-writhing, weeping Jack Chappell. 'And he cannot hate only in his heart, he must turn that hate into actions. This is a man who has persecuted you out of hate – hate for who you are, hate for what you are. For him, sex is only a way of using for his own gratification those he despises. He despises women in general, you in particular. What is the opposite of hate?'

'Love,' Miranda replied automatically. She was dreadfully afraid of where this was leading, yet she still lusted after Malachi. All she wanted was to feel his body moving over hers, his hands on her breasts. She wanted him inside her – *now*. She reached behind her, fumbled for the zip and slid it down. One shrug and the dress was around her ankles. The night was now bitterly cold but she barely noticed.

Malachi smiled and shook his head. 'No, that won't happen. I apologise for the effect my presence has on you. It affects everyone that way, men and women alike. The more time you spend around me, the stronger it gets. Did you see the way that waiter was looking at me? I really wish I could do something about it. I mean, it's not even as if I could reciprocate. I simply don't have the equipment. I wasn't made that way. My father has a bit of a thing about sex. He's very disapproving. And jealous. That's why I left his service and set up on my own. In my book, hate is an equal opportunities crime. I got a bit fed up with smiting Assyrians and Egyptians just because my father was convinced anyone who wasn't a Jew hated his chosen people by default. Mind you, he wasn't entirely wrong about that, was he? Anyway, the simple fact is that I have no *membrum virile*, so I won't be much use to you in that department.'

Miranda unclasped her bra and removed it. 'I don't bloody care,' she gasped as the cold air enveloped her nipples, now so erect it was almost painful. 'So you don't have a dick. You've got fingers and a tongue, haven't you?'

Malachi paused in the act of soaking a piece of rag in petrol. He seemed surprised, puzzled. 'You know, I honestly hadn't considered that. I suppose I owe you something – well, something other than this.' He gestured at Jack, who was moaning in terror. 'Actually, I've always felt a bit guilty about leaving my customers – ah – not *entirely* satisfied. Yes, why not? Never let it be said that this old dog can't learn a new trick. And while I may not be fully male I do have other – um – *attributes* that might be of interest.' He took out the Bic lighter, ignited the rag and held it out to her. 'But first, if you'd care to do the honours?'

Pop!

A forced smile, a futile hand signal to the children already passing her as she stopped in the middle of the road and held up the sign. A driver sounded his horn. A loud, male voice angrily shouted something about not having all effing day. She glanced at him as she hurriedly followed the last child to the kerb. If it was true that dogs resembled their owners, it was odds-on that this man kept a Staffie.

As he drove past in his white van, unnecessarily sounding the horn, a gust of wind hurled cold rain into her face and caught the lollipop, almost wrenching it from her hands. She gazed heavenward. The sky was as grey and grim as her mood.

Forty-one years, rain or shine, hot or cold, happy or sad. Always at the crossing at the stroke of eight to catch the early birds, never leaving until half past nine so the stragglers could reach their destination safely. Back again at three for another ninety-minute shift. Forty-one years. Forty-one sodding years.

It began when her own children had started school, in the days before parents had started taking their kids to the gates in big, four-wheel drive motors more appropriate for farmland and rural dirt tracks than suburban residential areas. In those days, most children still walked to school, alone or in groups, the younger ones accompanied by adults. With fewer vehicles on the road and the newspapers less fixated on stories of paedophile gangs, there had been rather less to worry about than now. But, like all mothers, at the back of her mind there had been the usual anxieties. Would the kids remember their Green Cross Code? Would they stick to zebra and pelican crossings? Would they take risks? Who would be looking out for them?

When she saw that advert in the local paper – school crossing patrol officers wanted – she didn't think twice. The pay wasn't exactly brilliant, but not too bad for a fifteen-hour week with no travel costs; and it was substantially better than the nothing she would earn as a housewife. It wasn't as if she was qualified to do much else. And it would be a sight better than being stuck in a factory or office all day doing repetitive work for an ungrateful boss. Plenty of fresh air, hours that would leave her ample time for her hobbies and the housework, doing something socially useful, having some involvement in ensuring her own children's well-being in their most vulnerable years – the more she thought about it, the more it appealed to her. She applied, was accepted, and found herself working at the busy crossroads between her home and the local primary school, no more than five hundred yards away. A brisk walk there and back twice a day, that would help her keep in trim.

That first day had been heavenly. A bright, warm day in late summer, small children laughing as she conducted them across the road, proud in her white and yellow reflective coat and peaked cap, brandishing the lollipop like a talisman – even the drivers had smiled and waved politely as she first held them up, then allowed them to pass. She got to know most of the youngsters, many of their parents, people she might otherwise never have known. She made friends. She was liked. She was respected. It was wonderful. The school term seemed to go by so quickly, but that didn't matter. There would be another, then another, and so many more. Forty-one fucking years.

The rot had set in gradually. The children became fewer, ruder. Their parents rarely walked with them, most too lazy to use their legs, preferring to drive their ridiculously oversized cars as close to the school as possible. Over the years, motorists' patience and courtesy eroded. The council privatised the school crossing patrol service, and she had been forced to reapply for her job, her pay slashed to the minimum wage. She had to pay for her own uniform. The local bus service had also been contracted out, to some cowboy operation that whittled down the timetable so that its buses were driven like bats out of hell by men and women who risked the sack if they failed to arrive at stops at the appointed time, meaning she had to make sure a bus wasn't due before stepping out into the road, otherwise she'd probably be flattened. Worse still, she was now in her sixties and bad weather played havoc with her arthritis. Some days were a physical torment.

The truth was, she no longer enjoyed the job she'd once loved. She went to work because she needed the money, even the pittance her new employers so reluctantly parted with once a month. Her husband, dead these last eight years, hadn't been what you'd call a saver and the life insurance had been swallowed up by funeral costs and legal fees. Her son's concern didn't stretch as far as his extra-deep pockets; and her daughter, having disappeared to Australia with a minor airline executive, only ever phoned at Christmas and on her birthday. Life was hard, money was tight, work was horrible. Some days, the weather and routine abuse made her so angry she felt as if she might burst with it all, popping like a balloon that had been over-inflated and stuck with a pin.

On this particular day, the weather was very bad. Her joints ached. Road users seemed uniformly at loggerheads with the world in general. She'd already been called a 'fucking old slag' by an aggressive, shaven-headed man in a white van who appeared to be more concerned with getting to work on time than the danger to life and limb he was posing by driving without regard to either the law or the Highway Code. She'd been insulted and sworn at by umpteen children, and had dutifully picked up and binned the trails of litter they left in their wake. And now there was another group of half a dozen or so foul-mouthed, bad-mannered brats approaching the crossing. She'd seen them before, almost every day for the last few weeks, but didn't know their names. Unusually, this surly troop of pre-teens was accompanied by an adult – a slouching, shell-suited, pony-tailed girl who didn't look old enough to be a mother but had probably given birth to at least two of the kids she was doing very little to supervise, her attention focused solely on her mobile phone. The kids were arguing, swearing, pinching and hitting one another, but the young woman didn't appear to notice, though every now and then she'd half-heartedly instruct them to 'fucking pack it in'.

One of the children, a little boy no more than seven years old, with tiny, pig-like eyes, stuck his middle finger up at her as they drew near.

She held her tongue and struggled to keep her temper, reminding herself that she needed the money. She even found a smile from somewhere. Miraculously, they stayed obediently by her side while she waited for the traffic to ease up. As they waited, she heard a hiss and a snigger and realised that a small girl had opened a can of Coca Cola and was spraying the frothy liquid all over her lower legs. The boy who'd given her the finger laughed then spat on her reflective coat. The woman nominally in charge of these goblins finally noticed what was going on, but chose only to take issue with the expression on the lollipop lady's face. 'They're only little kids,' she snapped, before a word had been said. 'You say one fucking word and I'll give you a slap, you poxy old bag.'

She turned away. The traffic had cleared for a moment. She marched into the road, face bright red with anger and shame, planted the lollipop firmly on the wet road and held up a hand, commanding oncoming traffic to stop. The first vehicle was the white van driven by the belligerent man who reminded her of a bull terrier. He'd been talking on his mobile phone and almost didn't stop, only slamming on the brakes at the very last second. He wasn't a happy man. 'Are you fucking still here?' he shouted. 'You got nothing better to do than fucking stand there stopping people trying to make a living? If you was a geezer, I'd get out of this motor and give you a right fucking kicking. Get them bastard kids across and be fucking quick about it.'

She ignored him and beckoned to the indignant woman and her unpleasant children to cross. The little boy now stuck two fingers up at her. She supposed it might be the nearest he ever got to developing a wide vocabulary. The girl threw the now-empty Coke can into the road and kicked it hard, straight into the lollipop lady's knee.

The pain was so intense that time seemed to stand still. The children were discarding sweet wrappers as they crossed. The mother was staring vacantly at that damned phone. The white van man was shouting more threats and obscenities. White heat spread from her knee, every other swollen, painful joint flaring in a chorus of sympathy. The balloon of anger expanded, its surface tight and fragile as the pressure continued to build.

Biting her lip against the pain, she glanced at her watch. In a few seconds it would be precisely seventeen minutes past nine. She bent down to talk to the horrid little boy. 'Would you like to hold my lollipop for a minute?' He nodded, those piggy eyes momentarily growing big and round. The mother, at first puzzled as to why they had all abruptly stopped, laughed. 'Bless,' she said. Then, suspiciously, 'Here, hang on a minute, it isn't heavy, is it?'

'No,' said the lollipop lady. 'They used to be, but now they're made of plastic. Cheap rubbish. You know how it is, all these local government cuts. Right, are you holding on to that tightly? Good boy. I'll cross first then I'll tell you when to follow me.'

She walked to the opposite side of the road, the side closest to her home, and kept on walking, staring straight ahead. As her feet touched the kerb she heard the hiss of brakes, a screech as tyres skidded on wet tarmac, children's screams, the sound of metal encountering metal and flesh at speed. The number 27 bus was bang on time, exactly eighteen minutes past the hour, as the timetable demanded.

Pop!

Hot Love

'What am I going to do with you?' Melanie glared at her husband, her arms folded and eyes narrowed. He didn't reply, his attention seemingly fixed on yet another embarrassing body.

She didn't expect him to answer. In the last few years their conversation had been mostly restricted to a desultory grunt or two over breakfast, a couple of words at dinner, terse requests and reluctant responses, an intermittent exchange of trivia. Now it was completely one-sided. There he was, propped up on the sofa in front of reality television shows while she pretended not to watch. It wasn't much of a marriage. Everything she'd enjoyed about it had dribbled away to nothing over time – the sex went stale sooner than she'd expected, their interests diverged, the pleasure they once took in each other's company decayed. He became dull with work and flabby with rest; she grew bored with him and restless at home. Not that he noticed, that combined company man and couch potato. When he wasn't thinking about work he was thinking of nothing at all.

She heaved a deep sigh. 'What's the point of talking to you? You're not even listening.'

It didn't help that she was seeing another man on the sly, a married colleague, though it was not so much an affair as an irregular series of snatched fumbles in the office stationery cupboard and the occasional satisfying but uncomfortable shag in the back of his car when she was supposed to be working late or out with friends. Not that she needed to maintain such fictions. But she felt obscurely guilty and compelled to make excuses to her unresponsive spouse, even though he was past caring what she got up to in the back of that BMW, or that she returned home reeking of another man's aftershave and bodily fluids.

The fact that her husband had been dead for nearly two months was another barrier to both marital harmony and meaningful conversation.

If Melanie was honest, waking up that morning to find him lifeless next to her in bed had been something of a relief. But if she was honest, she would have called an ambulance or the police, not phoned his employer to say he was sick and wouldn't be in for a while. If she was honest, she wouldn't have escalated his supposed sickness from a touch of 'flu to suspected ebola and possible intestinal cancer in the course of a month, and she would have been anxious about ignoring the increasingly frequent demands for doctor's notes and health bulletins. And if she was honest she wouldn't have continued to take money from his bank account via the cash dispenser at the bottom of the road and salt it away in her own. Honest women didn't behave that way.

She couldn't even say why she'd done it, not really. It was an impulse, something she'd done on the spur of the moment which had built up a momentum she felt unable to halt. At first she'd told herself it was because she was unable to accept he was dead, unable to bring herself to part from her dearly-loved husband. But she hadn't even been honest with herself. The truth, not buried very deeply, was that she was glad he was gone. His death meant that she could do what she wanted without worrying about him finding out. That mainly meant Harry at work, whose cheeky innuendo and saucy remarks were transparently an expression of lust that she was desperate to repay in kind. She'd sorted that on the very night of Gerald's death by accepting Harry's now-routine leering offer of a lift home for the very first time and getting shagged senseless in the litter-strewn car park of that empty factory near the railway sidings. Harry was a good-looking bloke, with a well-toned body that promised something special in terms of both size and stamina. Well, he hadn't disappointed and she was determined to get what she could from him until he lost interest. That was bound to happen. He was nearly twenty years her junior and his outlook on life was pretty immature for a married man with two young kids and a high-profile job, and just a little too pleased with himself for having an affair with an older woman. And Melanie had seen the way he looked at other women in the office. He'd trade her in for another bit on the side soon enough. In the meantime, she'd make the most of Harry the stallion. For that kind of pleasuring she was willing to overlook his roving eye, his occasional silliness and his smoking.

Sometimes Melanie wondered if her husband, wherever he was, knew about Harry. If there was an afterlife, did it offer the dead a window on the world they'd departed? And did they still care?

Her husband wasn't exactly out of sight but he was pretty much out of mind. Sometimes she couldn't even remember his name. Jerome, Jeremy, George – eventually she'd settle on Gerald, though a couple of times she'd had to check his wallet to be sure. It didn't really matter, unless his employer or his mother phoned. He was gone, and that was that.

Moving him around the house wasn't easy, even if he was a small man – in more ways than one, she reminded herself – and it was always hard to decide where to put him at any given moment. Still, he was better company now as he'd ever been when he was alive. At least now he didn't answer back when she scolded him. Now she did all the talking and he didn't say anything. He made less mess and created no laundry. She was no longer forced to put up with football and cricket on the television. It made life easier.

Melanie was eager to invite Harry round so they could indulge themselves in her marital bed. Shagging in the back of his car was all very well – and she wouldn't deny that having sex in public places added a certain thrilling edge to the proceedings – but she was fed up with rhythmically banging her head on the doors and windows, getting cramp, and struggling to remove and replace undergarments in such a confined space. And it was always done in such a bloody rush, despite Harry's proven staying-power. She yearned for room and time to fully experience his physical attributes. But if she did make her kingsize bed available to Harry for a night of unbridled lust, what on earth could she do with her dead husband?

The spare room was crammed full of junk. The other rooms were in use. The garage was a possibility but it was infested with mice and wasps had made a nest in one corner, which Gerald had been too lazy to sort out despite her nagging. She didn't like to go in there. Maybe she could wait until dark and drag him out to the garden shed, though that was pretty cluttered and she'd need to remove a lot of tools, a lawnmower and a wheelbarrow, and that would mean finding somewhere else to put them. If she left them piled up in the garden overnight without using them, the neighbours might suspect something was up. She didn't think Harry would be impressed if he turned up to find the kitchen or lounge filled with homeless gardening equipment. Even her sexiest lingerie and a large whisky might not distract him from that.

Gerald had been dead for nearly two days before she realised she had a big problem. He would decay. He would stink. There would be mess, maggots, flies. Melanie hated flies. And besides, she wasn't getting much sleep on the sofa. She really had to sort something out. But she couldn't call anyone now. What could she say? That she'd been away somewhere, on holiday or at a conference? There were plenty of witnesses to place her at work for those two days. No, it was too late to own up. The authorities might even think she was crazy. But what should she do? Dump the body somewhere and hope for the best? But she didn't drive and had never learned, always too afraid of other drivers to risk getting behind a steering wheel. And she couldn't exactly ask Harry to help her out. She was under no illusions there.

It was one of the older men at work who'd given her the idea, reminiscing about going to see the Tutankhamun exhibition at the British Museum in 1972, when he was in his late teens. It was blindingly obvious, really. She would embalm him. A Google search suggested it was ridiculously easy – all she needed was some embalming fluid, a strong pump, and a large bucket. Most of what she needed was in the shed. Gerald had routinely – and possibly illegally – used formaldehyde to disinfect their large fish tank and as a general fungicide, and there were a couple of gallons stored in a plastic storage box at the back of the garden, along with other flammable liquids. Somewhere in the shed was a pump Gerald used to empty the pond for cleaning. There were buckets under the kitchen sink and another by the tap in the side alley. Then there was Gerald's home brew equipment – a large barrel and what were surely yards of plastic tubing. Everything else could be improvised from kitchen utensils and Gerald's well-stocked but rarely-used toolbox.

She washed and dried Gerald's body in the bathroom, and sealed his anus with superglue. Then she hauled him downstairs and into the kitchen, panicking briefly when she realised she hadn't closed the blinds. The long dining table – one of Gerald's conceits – was already covered with plastic sheeting. Lifting him onto it was easier than she thought. Well, why not? She'd done most of the hard work around the house, certainly a damned sight more than Gerald, the lazy sod. It was really no wonder she was turning out to be stronger than she thought. The pump was ready, connected to Gerald's femoral artery – she hoped – with a plastic tube and a wide-aperture syringe once used for refilling printer cartridges. The embalming fluid was ready – formaldehyde mixed with a couple of bottles of rum and half a pint of nail varnish remover. Another tube, improvised from a plastic drinking straw and a cake icer, led from her husband's jugular vein to the beer barrel. She wore a half-mask respirator and goggles, and had two buckets, a mop and a pair of Marigold gloves standing by in case anything went wrong.

First, she took a good, sharp carving knife, slit him open from sternum to navel, and siphoned out the liquid contents of his abdominal cavity. Then she did the same with his large intestine, ridding him of digested food. After that she gave him an enema, then a final rinse with neat formaldehyde. When he was, as far as she could tell, internally spotless, she packed the gaping cavity with cotton wool and sewed him up. Now came the tricky part – the actual embalming.

It worked like a dream. The makeshift embalming fluid dissolved and forced the coagulated blood from Gerald's body and into the barrel. The change was clearly visible in the outlet's transparent tubing. When all the blood was out, Melanie stopped the pump. She sealed the hole in Gerald's neck with superglue, had a cup of tea while she waited for it to dry, then restarted the pump to force a little more embalming fluid into the corpse. When that was done she applied more glue to the hole in his neck, poured some of the fluid into his mouth and stitched it shut.

As an afterthought, she shaved Gerald's head – not that there was much to come off – and gave him a couple of all-over coats of marine varnish that had been kept with the formaldehyde. It couldn't hurt, and she was a bit concerned that the softer external tissues might not take with the formaldehyde mixture. By the next morning he was dry, set and ready to be moved and posed. For decency's sake – but mostly so she wouldn't have to see his shrivelled penis dangling uselessly every time she moved him – she dressed him in his favourite clothes and a pair of Adidas trainers. He would have liked that. The expelled blood and abdominal juices went on the flower beds, which would also have pleased him, even if the solvent content did seem to be slowly killing the roses.

When it was all over and she was relaxing in the cleaned-up kitchen with a large glass of wine, Melanie allowed herself a delighted laugh. She'd embalmed her husband for a total outlay of around sixty pounds, and all of that had come from Gerald's surprisingly healthy bank account. It hadn't even been as gross as she'd feared – not much different from preparing a chicken for the oven. She thought she'd have made a damned good undertaker.

At first she was pleased with her handiwork, though a certain amount of snagging was needed. Despite the stitches his mouth kept falling open, so she superglued that shut, just as she'd done with his arse, feeling a little guilty that Gerald would no longer be able to enjoy what seemed to have become his main pleasures in life – taking in food and expelling it as both solid and gaseous waste when its job was done. Then his disconcertingly sinking eyelids had to be hidden by a pair of cheap sunglasses. If it wasn't for his utter silence, ultra-glossy, yellowish skin and the smell of chemicals, inadequately masked by air-freshener, anyone would think he was still alive. It wasn't as if he was any less lively now, was it?

Now, though, she was stuck with him. Even if she did somehow manage to take him somewhere else, he might be found and identified. The police would visit, the pathologist would see Gerald had been embalmed, and questions would be asked. She couldn't even plead innocence. Embalming your husband wasn't exactly something you could do by accident, was it? They would have her bang to rights for concealing a death – and they might even suspect her of causing Gerald's demise. The embalming might be seen as an attempt to destroy evidence. Worse still, the longer she kept him around, the more difficult it would be to keep up the increasingly elaborate pretence that he was still in the land of the living. Her dead husband may in theory have been a bit of company, no matter how inadequate; but he was also a liability.

Gerald stared blankly at the television screen, where medical prurience had given way to a programme about people getting ready for a wedding. When Melanie and Gerald married, they'd kept it simple and informal. Not these characters. Everyone involved, male and female, was going well over the top – horse-drawn carriages, matching livery, yards of bling, insanely expensive clothing, far too much make-up. It was amazing how much time, energy and money some people spent to look so tacky, tasteless and cheap. The women used so much hair spray that it would be dangerous to light a cigarette within a fifty-yard radius of any one of them. When the limousines came to take them to church, the combination of petrol and flammable polymers would put their entire street at risk. One spark and…

Of course! That was how she could get rid of the evidence and get Gerald out of her hair once and for all. Burn the body. She wouldn't need much accelerant. With all that formaldehyde, rum and solvent soaked into his tissues, not to mention the varnish, Gerald would burn like a torch. Melanie's mind raced. Within five minutes, she had a plan.

First, she sent Harry a text message. *R u up 4 it 2nite*

He replied almost immediately. *2 rt. Whr + whn*

My plce. G away til 2mrrw. C u @ 8 x

U bet x

Melanie didn't know why they exchanged texts so often, when colleagues in their line of work phoned each other all the time as a matter of routine. No one would suspect anything was going on, certainly not Harry's wife, who Melanie had met once and thought was a bit dozy. Harry had started it – invitations to assignations at first, then lurid descriptions of what he wanted to do to her, all in that odd macaronic language of abbreviation, acronym and shorthand favoured by the young. Only last week he had texted her a photograph of his erect penis with a red ribbon tied around it in a bow. It was another sign of his immaturity. Still, she could overlook his childish habits if it meant she'd get a good seeing-to out of it. And that photograph had certainly made her hot to trot that night.

The garage was the obvious place to solve the Gerald problem. A solid brick and concrete structure with metal doors, it would contain the blaze and most of the smoke. By the time anyone noticed the smoke and called the fire brigade, Gerald would be well and truly cooked. Bugger the mice and good riddance to the wasps. Quickly, she wrapped Gerald in a sheet and carried him out of the house, through the back garden and into the garage by its side door. Gerald's car, as usual was unlocked. She hauled the body into the driver's seat and pulled the seat belt across the chest to keep it upright. Then she went to the storage box at the far end of the garden and ferried an assortment of boxes, bottles and cans back to the garage and into the car – paraffin, turpentine, white spirit, perchlorethylene, varnish, weedkiller – and loosened the caps on all that contained a liquid. With the petrol in the nearly-full tank, that cocktail should muddy the waters sufficiently to deflect attention from her. The chemicals in Gerald's body would barely register. If asked, she would say Gerald had planned to take the stuff to the nearby council depot for safe disposal. Unfortunately, he must have decided to put fuel in his cigarette lighter before he set off. Clumsy old Gerald must have spilled some and lit up without noticing.

The only snag was that Gerald didn't smoke. But that wasn't much of a problem. She could say he'd recently taken up smoking because he'd been under stress arising from his undiagnosed illness. Yes, that was it. She would go down to the newsagent on the corner and make some casual remark to that effect while she was buying a lighter, liquid fuel and cigarettes. What sort of cigarettes would Gerald have smoked, if he'd smoked? Something dull and ordinary, she supposed. Marlboro were ordinary. But were they dull enough for Gerald? Probably not. He'd go for something boring but not too down-market. Mayfair King Size or whatever.

She'd need to work out how to ignite her husband and get out of the garage before joining him in the inferno, but that could wait until tomorrow. Right now, she wanted an evening of good, hot sex, the dirtier the better. Coughing as a mixture of volatile fumes began to seep from the car, she closed the garage door and went back into the house. Now she had to get ready for Harry. She had time to vacuum up the flakes of skin and dried varnish Gerald had shed during this latest move, change the bedding, take a leisurely bath, and get dried and dressed before he was due to arrive. The new Victoria's Secret underwear, a couple of squirts of that Chanel she'd treated herself to when Harry started to show an interest. She wouldn't be needing much more than that tonight but she decided something ought to be worn on top, just in case one of the neighbours spotted her opening the door practically naked to a strange man. In the end she opted for her black silk kimono – comfortable, attractive yet outwardly respectable, and easily removed.

At five to eight, she was just applying sinfully-scarlet lipstick when her phone rang. It was him.

'Harry? Where are you?' She was almost breathless with anticipation.

'I'm at your place. Thought I'd have a quick ciggie before we get started. I know you're not keen on smoking – thought you wouldn't appreciate me doing it in the house.'

She moved the bedroom curtain to one side and looked down at the front of the house. It was raining heavily and there was no one in sight. 'But I can't see you. Are you still in your car?'

He laughed. 'No, I noticed your garage and popped inside to get out of the rain. Can't find the light switch so I'm treading carefully. I must say, it really stinks of something in here. Smells like chemicals. With that pong, at least old Gerald won't notice any lingering smoke. I'll see you in five minutes. Just lighting up now –'

A Bad Apple

'Christ, I don't fucking care.' She was bored with the conversation. It had been dragging on for nearly five minutes, three minutes longer than her attention-span could handle. Her father stood there, helplessly wondering what he could do to make this ancient child see reason, or how he could make her understand his concerns, if she understood the seriousness of what she had done. Thirteen year old girls weren't like they were when he was a kid; and in those days they hadn't been much like they were when his parents were kids. This petite creature sitting sullenly on her bed amid a chaos of clothing, cosmetics and magazines might as well have been a visitor from another world.

'Don't use that sort of language,' he protested, knowing how lame it must have sounded to her. When he'd been a boy he would never have dared to swear in front of his mum and dad. Nowadays it was *de rigueur*.

She stared at him incredulously. 'Fuck off, Dad – what's wrong with the way I speak?'

He didn't dare to answer, fearful that another wrong word could set her off. The last tantrum had resulted in broken crockery and windows, and a ruined iPod. Instead, he sighed and sat cautiously on the edge of the bed. With her and all the mess already on it there was just about room to perch one of his buttocks. 'I'm really worried about you, Billie,' he told her. 'It's so risky, what you're doing. It could ruin your life if you're not careful. And what you've done – well, it's serious. It's really bad.'

She rolled her eyes and gave him one of those looks that women give men who have fallen short of expectations. Thirteen going on thirty, he thought. Billie was old beyond her years, mentally at least. But her body was still growing and he knew for sure that somewhere inside her there was still a vulnerable child. There was a place in her make-up where hormones, peer pressure, attitude and emotion met but did not mesh, like an unholy Venn diagram with a volatile centre. It was the place where her frequent explosions originated.

He gazed distractedly around her bedroom. There were still soft toys and pink ornaments acquired when she was much younger, Hello Kitty and My Little Pony dotted here and there like fossils exposed in fractured rock. A poster of a dead American rapper hung next to her wardrobe, a warning he should perhaps have heeded. 'We care about you, me and your mother. If anything happened to you – well, I don't even like to think about it.'

Billie snorted derisively. 'You two don't care about me. All you care about is your own feelings. If anything bad did happen to me you'd just worry about what other people thought of you and feel sorry for yourselves.'

'That isn't true,' he told her, knowing even as he said it that it was the wrong thing. She'd laid the trap and he'd walked right into it. There would be nothing rational or logical about what came next; but reason didn't belong in this situation. Her eyes blazed with fury.

'Are you calling me a liar?'

'Of course not,' he said, in as soothing a tone as he could manage. Not that it mattered. The conversation had already slid over the edge of conciliation and was now freefalling into the abyss. 'But you know we care about you. Come on, Billie – give me a break here.'

She was having none of it. Her lower lip quivered and her eyes began to water. He'd been here before and knew exactly how this was going to play out. *It isn't fair.*

'It isn't fair,' she sobbed. *You've never trusted me.* 'You've never trusted me.' *You treat me like a child.* 'You treat me like a child.' *I wish I'd never been born.* 'I wish I'd never been born.'

The same stock phrases, rolled out again and again, paraded every time she thought she might not get her own way. Well, it wasn't going to work this time. Suddenly he saw himself as she did: a soft touch, a weak man who would agree to anything she wanted to keep the peace, even this.

No, not this – this was something he simply couldn't allow, even if the result was going to be years of misery. Her feelings were one thing but he couldn't agree to this. He could put up with his daughter being stupid or selfish – but this was quite simply wrong. She was asking him and her mother to connive at something that was both criminal and morally repugnant. The fact that she'd already done it – and that tacitly he'd as good as agreed to help her cover it up – was neither here nor there. In that moment he almost hated her for what she was forcing him to do.

'You *are* a child,' he snapped, furious at the attempted manipulation. 'You're thirteen years old and you know nothing about the world. You act as if you don't even understand that you've committed a criminal act and someone got hurt while you were doing it. The only reason I haven't called the police is that I don't want to see you interrogated about it. These things you're doing – you and your friends – it's got to stop.'

The look she gave him nearly broke his heart, a venomous glare that combined hatred and contempt in equal measure. 'Oh yeah? How do you plan on stopping us? What are you going to do, lock me up?'

'No,' he said quietly. 'But you're grounded until further notice and I'm taking your laptop and phone. I'll be checking our outgoing landline calls and I'll lock my office so you can't use my PC. If you call them or they try to contact you, I *will* call the police. Do you understand me?'

That was enough. He stood, collected her laptop and iPhone, and left the room. Even as the door was closing he heard a scream and the sound of objects being thrown as she vented her rage.

It was still going on an hour later. By now she must have destroyed everything in her room that could be broken. Her voice rose regularly as she found new terms of abuse and hate, interspersed with blood-chilling screams. This was her worst tantrum ever. At this rate it wouldn't be long before the neighbours cracked and either came knocking at their or phoned the police. And then it would all come out. He said as much to Lorraine.

'Maybe that would be for the best,' his wife suggested. 'I know you want to do the right thing for her, but perhaps keeping quiet isn't the way. We can't just pretend it hasn't happened, can we? Maybe we should just call the police ourselves and tell them what we know.'

'I can't put her through that,' he insisted. 'She'd be questioned by the police and might even have to go to court. Shit, they might even lock her up. It'd be a terrible ordeal and she'd never forgive us.'

'Look, she isn't going to forgive us no matter what we do. We'll be as much in the wrong for telling the police as we are for stopping her seeing those bloody vermin. And if she keeps on doing it and gets caught, that'll be our fault too. She blames us for everything. Besides, what she's done is horrible. It's bad enough her stealing from us and bunking off school but this is too much.'

'But we can't grass on our own child. She's really still only a little girl, isn't she?'

He was pleading and knew how pathetic it sounded. Lorraine opened her mouth as if to speak but stopped and turned away. It didn't go unnoticed. He became defensive.

'What is it?'

'It isn't just her, is it? What about her sisters? If they know what she's been doing and not been punished for it, what kind of example are we setting them? How can we let her get away with it?'

She was right. He had no answer that would satisfy those questions. Upstairs the noise rose to a crescendo of screams, foul language and the sound of things being broken.

'Besides,' she continued, her voice dropping to a whisper, 'besides, she's even worse when you're not here. There's something seriously wrong with the girl. She's unbearable. If you think this is bad now, you have no bloody idea just how bad she can be. I don't think I can take any more of her. I know she's only a kid but I can't live with her anymore. Either Billie goes or I do.'

It was getting dark. Standing on the pavement outside the house, he looked up at the silhouette passing rapidly back and forth across her bedroom window. The noise was increasing as her rage continued to scale new heights. It wouldn't be long before one of the neighbours picked up the phone and called the police. He might as well save them a job, and in so doing save his marriage while destroying forever what little remained of his relationship with his eldest daughter.

And Lorraine was right: Billie would be a dreadful influence on Hannah and Sophie as they grew up. She was a bad apple. And she might even harm them in other ways. The stolen goods Lorraine had found stashed in a cupboard confirmed that – smartphones, credit cards, jewellery, a couple of purses and, worst of all, the wallet of an old man who had lived a few streets away until a few weeks earlier someone had broken into his home one night, tied him up and tortured him until he revealed his Visa and MasterCard PINs, then left him to choke on his own blood. An old man treated brutally and left to die by Billie and her friends, for only a couple of hundred quid. It was a minor miracle that he had survived, albeit in such a state that he was still in hospital and wasn't expected to recover enough to be able to return to his home. What if Billie had been responsible for the violence? Her destructive rages suggested that she was more than capable of that. And could she be trusted not to hurt her younger siblings?

He took a long drag on the cigarette he'd cadged from Lorraine, his first for six years, and flipped open the scuffed clamshell phone. The local police station's number was on speed-dial, the legacy of a recent residents' association meeting at which a neighbourhood copper had confided that it would generate a much faster response than dialling 999. As he pressed the call button, he heard a scream and the sound of breaking glass. He didn't even have time to look up – before he could so much as twitch a single muscle she slammed headfirst into the paved forecourt immediately below her window, accompanied by a shower of glittering shards that shattered into crystals as they too struck the concrete slabs.

Numb with shock, he stared at his daughter's body, the eyes in that splintered skull wide and vacant, fixed forever on an infinity he could not imagine. She seemed tiny, a broken elf in a spreading pool of liquid ruby scattered with icy diamonds. A small, tinny voice was asking barely-audible questions from something clutched in his right hand. His front door opened and Lorraine came rushing out, emitting a sob as loud as one of Billie's recent screams as she saw what had happened, ran to her child and began with frantic, heart-rending futility to attempt resuscitation.

He was paralysed with the horror of what had just happened. He felt his own scream struggling to ascend from the pit of his stomach as the scene unfolded before his horrified gaze like the final act of a Greek tragedy. Yet, like a piece of *Grand Guignol* theatre, somehow it was so gruesome and shocking that he couldn't take it entirely seriously, and the struggle between grief and disbelief left him numb, his mind as immobilised as his body. Stupidly, all he could think was that even the bad apple didn't fall far from the tree.

Bullshit Detector

'What's that?' I asked. My Uncle Ron had been busy with scissors, a soldering iron and a tube of superglue. The kitchen table was littered with bits and pieces.

He held his creation up so I could get a good look at it. It was a cardboard cube, about six inches to a side. On the top he'd glued a cone, also made from cardboard but lined on the inside with baking foil. The mouth of the cone projected an inch or so over the edge of the cube. A plastic straw, one of those ones with a bendy bit like a concertina, fed from the pointed end through a hole in the cube's upper face. There was another hole in the bottom, through which a yard or so of copper wire dangled. The whole assemblage, apart from the foil and the wire, had been painted black.

'It's a Bullshit Detector,' he said, turning it round. That's when I saw the third hole, into which a torch bulb was set.

'A what?'

'A Bullshit Detector,' he repeated. Uncle Ron wasn't normally quite so patient, but from the smell and the roaches in his ashtray, I suspected he was pretty stoned. A couple of spliffs and a full belly always put him in a good mood.

'Bullshit,' I scoffed, and was amazed to see the bulb light up. As far as I could see he hadn't done anything to make it do that.

He grinned triumphantly through his untidy facial hair. 'See? It works.'

Uncle Ron was a bit of hippie. Well, to be honest, he was quite a lot of a hippie. Sixty-one years old, he weighed in at around twenty-two stone, had a ratty beard and greying brown hair hanging halfway down his back in a ponytail but receding at the front. He habitually dressed in a purple or yellow t-shirt, one of several paisley waistcoats, and flared blue jeans. Not only did Ron look the part, he talked the talk. He had tales of hanging out in the Grove with heads and freaks, going to demos and free concerts, sit-ins and squats, getting his head together in the country, and lots of other things no one I knew could translate. Even my mum – Ron's younger sister – didn't know what he was on about most of the time. He'd lived with us for as long as I could remember, nominally in a small bedroom next to mine, though he'd eventually annexed the conservatory and one of the two garden sheds, where he spent most of his time. Everywhere he spent more than a few seconds reeked for days afterwards of patchouli, sandalwood and cannabis.

To the best of my knowledge Ron never did a day's real work in his life – 'the Man' was his avowed if vague and undefined enemy and working for the Man was out of the question – content to live on state benefits, small profits from buying and selling old records on eBay, and the sometimes grudging generosity of family and friends. I always suspected Ron's detestation of the Man, the Rat Race and White Middle Class Male Supremacy in general masked a genuine fear of exerting himself. I never knew him to leave the house more than once a week, when he would amble ponderously to the shops just down the road, withdraw some money from his bank account, and stock up on tobacco, Rizlas, snacks and materials for his machines. Everything else he needed came by mail order, or he'd get one of us to get it. As a hippie, Uncle Ron also walked the walk, but it was never very far.

I'm not so sure that Ron was just a lazy sod, though. He was more the creative type. I've mentioned his machines. He made lots of them. Maybe 'machines' isn't the right word because none had any moving parts, but that's what he called them so we all went along with it. There was a foot-high cardboard pyramid built to the exact angles and proportions of the Great Pyramid of Giza, which he claimed kept his razor blades sharp. I suppose it may well have done, not that he ever shaved. Then there was the device made from three tape-sealed shoe boxes glued in a triangular formation on a sheet of plywood. The front two were mounted with the bare metal halves of a set of bicycle handlebars. Wires led from these boxes to the third, which had two dials drawn on the lid in blue and red felt pen respectively. The dials read from one to thirteen clockwise, and the needles were glued permanently at the seven mark. This, Ron asserted, kept him balanced. Every evening at sunset he would grasp the handles, close his eyes, and balance himself. I don't know if it had any real effect but I must say he was always a bit grumpy on summer evenings.

The best machine was something he called an Interdimensional Transporter. This was a sheet of cardboard lined on the inside with CDs glued with the shiny sides facing in – he favoured CDs of old Jimi Hendrix albums, 'for the vibes' – and those flexible adhesive mirrors you can get from Poundland. Ron would smoke a couple of spliffs, fit the Interdimensional Transporter over his head and sit directly under a naked light bulb. He reckoned it was just like Doctor Who's TARDIS – bigger on the inside – and had similar abilities to take him through space and time. I tried it once. All I could see was my own face and various parts of my head, distorted and reflected back at me countless times. It wasn't a pretty sight and it gave me a migraine. Maybe if I'd smoked some weed first it might have helped but I couldn't find Ron's stash. In all those years I never did.

The Bullshit Detector was impressive. OK, I was only fifteen, but even so. That evening we tried it out a few times. We sat and watched the news on Channel 4 with the machine on the coffee table and, sure enough, whenever a politician opened his or her mouth to speak, the bulb would light up. It flicked on and off during the commercial breaks, throughout *The Apprentice* and *I'm A Celebrity*, and only remained wholly unlit for the duration of *Guitar Heroes* on BBC4. I was amazed.

Late in the evening we retired to Ron's room and – for the first time ever – we shared a spliff, to the accompaniment of his scratched and worn copy of the Beatles' *White Album*. Vinyl, of course. Ron loathed CDs, which he reckoned leached the music's soul, though he was happy to use Hendrix CDs for other purposes, as I said earlier. He had a hefty stack of LPs, which he stored under a table. I flicked through them as we passed the joint back and forth. The Beatles, Rolling Stones, the Move, Doors, Jefferson Airplane, Grateful Dead, Tyrannosaurus Rex, Incredible String Band, Bob Dylan, Pink Floyd, Cream, Hendrix (of course) – an old hippie's desert island discs, nothing older than 1966 and not a lot later than 1972, when – according to Ron – 'They all started to sell out, man. Except for the ones that died.' His bookshelves echoed the time he'd become locked into. Timothy Leary, Mick Farren and Richard Neville rubbed spines with Herman Hesse, Tolkien and *Zen and the Art of Motorcycle Maintenance*.

When the spliff had been smoked down to the roach, I emerged from under the table, banging my head in the process, waving a stained and battered cover that I was sure contained an equally stained and battered LP. 'Never heard of this one,' I said.

He squinted at the cover. 'Man, that's one of my favourites. David Peel and the Lower East Side. Far out. You put it on the deck while I get the cheese puffs and crisps out. Then I'll skin up again. Bugger, I forgot to balance myself this evening. Oh well, fuck it, too late now.'

So we ate junk food, smoked a couple more spliffs, and listened and sang along to 'I Like Marijuana' and 'Up Against The Wall', ending the first side with happily stoned shouts of *motherfucker!*

And that's when I noticed the Bullshit Detector, sitting by the record turntable on Ron's psychedelically-painted chest of drawers that stood to the right of his bed. The light was glowing brightly. 'Ron,' I said, 'the light's been on all the way through this record.'

Ron was aghast. 'Oh, man – not David Peel. No fucking way. I thought that guy really meant it. No, that's too fucking much.' With an anguished moan he fell to his knees and began to rummage frantically through his LP collection.

Now the thing about Uncle Ron was that he really believed all that hippie stuff from the Sixties. Peace and love, flower-power, chakras and mantras, karma and dharma and Black Panthers – you name it and to Ron it was all true and self-evident. The late Sixties were humanity's lost chance at Paradise. He'd turned on, tuned in and dropped out to such a degree that he barely existed in what I considered the real world. Now he chose a selection of albums by, I guessed, artists representative of his ideals and began to play tracks at random. And every time a track began, the Bullshit Detector lit up; and the light winked out when the track ended and he lifted the stylus.

Record after record failed the test. I'd never seen him look so distraught, so lost. Then he played his trump card, his totem and talisman – a signed copy of *Electric Ladyland*. Uncle Ron, who claimed to have been at the Monterey Pop festival and Woodstock, and said he'd met Hendrix several times, starting with something called UFO in London in 1967, swore that at the exact moment Jimi died – he always referred to Hendrix solely as 'Jimi' – the record had floated through the air from a shelf and landed gently on his chest as he lay in bed. Naturally, I thought Ron had probably been tripping at the time, but you never know.

Reverently, he removed the treasured vinyl from its paper sleeve and laid it on the turntable. Seconds later, the opening notes of 'Burning of the Midnight Lamp' emanated from the speakers. The bulb on the Bullshit Detector glowed. Ron stood, open-mouthed and blank-eyed. Then he wept.

'Leave me alone, man,' he whispered as the tears coursed down his face and trickled into his beard. 'I'm really freaking out here and I need to be alone to get myself together.'

I opened my mouth to say something comforting, although quite honestly I had no idea what to say, but he shook his head. I nodded, offered him a rather stoned look of what I hoped would be taken for sympathy, and got out of there.

The next morning, Ron didn't come down for breakfast. When he still hadn't appeared by eleven, my mum went up to see if he was alright. He wasn't of course.

According to the post-mortem, Uncle Ron died of a heart attack. Our GP wasn't in the least surprised. Ron had been morbidly obese, took little exercise, and lived on junk food, cigarettes and weed. A myocardial infarction was only a matter of time; and that time had come. My mum was really upset. Well, he was her older brother, after all. I was fairly gutted myself. He might have been seriously weird but Ron was a good bloke and I liked him. He was more of a mate than an uncle. Mind you, I think my dad was secretly pleased. He'd been in the army and he had no time for long-haired layabouts. Dad and Ron had never seen eye to eye about anything.

It wasn't just a heart attack, of course. I found that out after the funeral when I came home before my parents and stretched out on Ron's bed. Right then, I found his characteristic scents comforting. It made me feel as if he hadn't really gone, that he was just on the bog or in the bath and would be in at any moment. Yeah, I know it sounds silly. But I was very upset and only fifteen years old, don't forget. Anyway, I lay there and shut my eyes and tried to remember him. I reached out and touched the record deck with the fingertips of my left hand. Then I realised *Electric Ladyland* was still on the turntable. I sat up and lifted the stylus onto the disc – it would be a fitting tribute. The Bullshit Detector lit up. And as I took my hand away my fingers brushed the case of the turntable and I received an almighty electric shock.

I used some words that would have caused even Uncle Ron to raise his eyebrows and took a closer look. The power cord was, by my estimation, about two feet shorter than it should have been and was patched here and there with insulating tape. Thinking about it, it made sense. I couldn't remember Ron ever buying wire, yet he used quite a lot of the stuff in his machines. This, I deduced, had been his source. The silly bugger must have messed up the connection somehow. When the turntable was powered on and the stylus moved to the 'play' position, the whole thing was live. Experimentally, I moved the Bullshit Detector away from the deck. The light went out. I moved it back and the light came on. Poor Ron had died miserable, for no good reason.

That was five years ago. I inherited Ron's library of hippie texts, his record collection and his assortment of non-moving machines. I passed on the clothes, though. The local clothing bank was welcome to them.

Sometimes, I smoke a bit of weed and put the

Interdimensional Transporter over my head. It doesn't take me anywhere. But I use the Bullshit Detector quite a lot. It still lights up whenever a politician speaks on the television or radio, and quite often when my dad says anything. I did consider taking it apart to see how it works, but I couldn't bring myself to do it. It just seemed wrong. It weighs about as much as you'd expect of a few bits of cardboard and wire and an old torch bulb, so there can't be any batteries in there. Anyway, how would it work? There are no switches, no controls of any kind. Static electricity, possibly – but if so, how does it do the detecting? Did Uncle Ron somehow imbue his machine with part of his own soul?

I've used the machine a lot lately. There's a General Election in a couple of weeks and I've been vetting the party political broadcasts, advertisements, debates and what have you. But so far everything I've seen or heard or read from any of them has been bullshit.

Tinsel

Usually, for me Christmas is a time of restful isolation, a couple of weeks spent reading, watching DVDs, listening to noisy rock music, and drinking. Anything that doesn't involve tinsel, pointy trees and wrapping paper, or saccharine-flavoured sentimentality – not to mention the annual one-night stand with religion, the spiritual equivalent of the kind of drunken, loveless tumble that leaves both parties disappointed and regretful. I hate Christmas.

How can anyone face this time of year sober? The syrupy sentiment soon turns to unnavigable sludge that stops you in your tracks and leaves you floundering helplessly in the supermarket aisles, barely able to continue that mindless seasonal spending orgy. Bing Crosby tells you of his monochrome dreams, Noddy Holder wishes you a merry one yet again, and Roy Wood goes on about the bloody bells ringing out for what must surely be the billionth time. Everywhere you look, you are blinded by glitter, lights and shiny baubles. It's like being held prisoner in Slade's *Top of the Pops* dressing room in 1973.

Inevitably, you abandon the desperate quest for that elusive appropriate gift for the loved one of your choice and head for the booze section to stock up on the real Christmas spirit.

And I know exactly how you feel. We're not talking of Dickensian ghosts here. I mean the real alcoholic deal – whisky, brandy, rum, vodka, gin, tequila – I don't care, just so long as it blots out the madness around me for a few days. The TV is mothballed for a month, the radio is sent to Coventry and the newspapers shunned. I take the week before Christmas off to avoid the desperate meals and overwrought parties, the ersatz *bonhomie* from people who would otherwise ignore me except to stab me in the back. Then I start drinking and don't stop until the first day of January, when the Baby Jesus is back in his pram and well on his way out of Bethlehem, New Year's Eve has been reduced to a mere headache, and the bills are being totted up.

My disenchantment with Christmas started twenty years ago, when I was thirty, out with friends on Christmas Eve. We had a good drink in our usual pub, the regular crowd and a few strangers, friends of friends. However, some of them weren't so friendly. Just before kicking-out time, one of my mates drunkenly kissed one of the other regulars, as he'd done several Christmases running. Unfortunately, this time the young woman had brought along a new boyfriend who didn't take kindly to such casual familiarity. Within seconds of the kiss, my pal was on the beer-sticky floor with what seemed like pints of blood spouting from a face that had been on the receiving end of a glass wielded not so much in anger as insane, homicidal fury. One of my other mates decked the assailant, whose friends set about him, and so on. The Saviour's birthday dawned with several people in hospital and quite a few of us helping the police with their enquiries. I was neither injured nor charged but still got home far too late to get my meagre bachelor's Christmas dinner started. I made do with a cheese sandwich and strawberry yoghurt before throwing in the towel and crashing out until Boxing Day, the evening of which was spent visiting my now disfigured and partially-sighted friend in hospital.

Until then I'd been a believer, not in the religious side of Christmas but in the idea of putting aside a time for people to have fun and be nice to one another. That night out destroyed my faith in the ideal. It wasn't really that much worse than previous Christmas piss-ups, except that before we had only been witnesses to alcohol-fuelled mayhem, usually sparked by petty jealousy when the seasonal kisses were being distributed. Maybe it was my personal involvement that got to me. Maybe it was the sight of my mate lying in a hospital bed with his face covered in bandages and learning that he would probably come out with a glass eye and a white stick. Or perhaps it was just my age, that magical thirty-year marker propelling me into sudden maturity. Whatever it was, I'd had enough. I thought back to all the Yuletide family rows – what happens when a disparate bunch of people connected only by blood and marriage are forced to co-exist in close confinement for several days amid exhaustion and worries about money – the pub brawls, the tearful women shouted at by enraged men solely because some other bloke was looking at them, the bickering drunks, the resentful coppers sorting out the aftermath of other people's stupidity. Peace on earth and goodwill to all men? Don't make me laugh.

After that I opted out of Christmas as far as I was able.

At work I went along with it for a while but soon sickened of cramped, elbow-knocking tables and unappetising food prepared in bulk and specially overpriced for the seasonal diner. In truth, Christmas in the workplace was as depressing as Yuletide Fight Club at the pub. Secret Santa was merely an excuse for bitching about colleagues' lack of imagination and tight-fistedness. Senior managers who didn't care if I lived or died wished me a merry Christmas and forgot who I was the minute they turned away. Chocolates and mince pies stacked up, a never-ending stream ferried in by people who seemed unable to stop spending and appeared hell-bent on eating themselves into the tomb. And every year, as the world grew more unpleasant and money became tighter, the worse it got. A few years ago, when the global economy was finally exposed as a shabby fraud no better than a mismanaged Ponzi scheme, it seemed to me that Christmas had genuinely turned into a period when by common agreement people were licensed to be insane. The less money they had, the more they spent. The more their lives crumbled around them, the happier they were determined to be. That was when I finally Grinched out. No more sodding Christmas for me. I vowed that from then on I would maintain a dignified, drunken solitude at this time of year. My sole concession was to send Christmas cards, no more than a dozen, to family and the few old friends I still cherish.

Two days ago it all changed.

I still have family back in my home town. We keep in touch. And that was why, on that rainy Christmas Eve, my comfortable routine was broken. I received a red-flagged e-mail from my detested cousin John, telling me my aunt had been taken ill. As far as family goes, Aunt Rachel had always been one of my favourites. Now in her late seventies, my father's sister was normally robust and healthy, so the sudden hospitalisation was worrying. My cousin intimated that Rachel might be suffering from cancer, though her symptoms – severe gastric pain, insomnia and general discomfort – could have fitted any one of a thousand ailments. I dutifully made myself presentable, boarded the tube to Liverpool Street and took the train east to my home town, hoping against hope that they hadn't made further cuts to the bus service at the other end.

My luck was out. The bus service had been discontinued, apparently because it wasn't making the megabucks every bloody businessman seems to expect from even the smallest operation nowadays, and I paid through the nose for a taxi to the hospital. If it hadn't been freezing cold and pissing with rain I would have walked, as it's only about a mile from the station. Naturally, when I arrived at the hospital, where the waiting area had been transformed into something resembling Roy Wood's make-up box, it was only to find that Aunt Rachel had been diagnosed with acute wind, probably caused by an excess of seasonal sprouts and pickles, and discharged. I briefly toyed with the idea of popping round to see her but decided to cut my losses and return to London.

By this time it was six in the evening on Christmas Eve, the peak time for panic shopping, and there were no taxis to be had for love or money. I was left with no choice but to get back to the station on foot, in the worsening rain and plummeting temperature. It was that or feigning illness to get a bed for the night, and incarceration with a bunch of genuinely sick people did not appeal. Besides, I had a cupboard filled with booze and the new Stephen King to get back to.

Bad news awaited me at the station. The incessant downpour had caused a landslip near Shenfield and all trains were cancelled until further notice. The station staff told me, with that insincerely sad shake of the head that is surely learned on special training courses, that the problem was highly unlikely to be sorted until the next morning. And there would be no trains the next morning because it was Christmas Day. I was stranded.

In an ideal world, I would have gone to stay with Aunt Rachel or her son, my cousin Nick, who's a pretty decent bloke. But Nick was now living in Scotland and Rachel was spending Christmas with John, whose wife and kids are precisely the kind of venal, selfish, squabbling specimens I prefer to avoid. The alternative was to try to find a hotel or bed and breakfast place for the next two nights, but I suspected that would be a difficulty too far. Anyway, I couldn't really afford it, having already lashed out on enough books and DVDs to keep me occupied over Christmas, and invested in a quantity of booze that would float the Ark Royal. The situation required some serious thought, and I needed a drink.

Just down the High Street from the station there was a pub I didn't remember from either my time living in the town or my more recent visits. It certainly looked new, and unlike most of the other boozers I'd passed there were no bouncers on the door and you didn't need a ticket to get in. I supposed it hadn't yet been in existence long enough to have acquired a regular client base. I think it had once been a bank or a betting shop, but couldn't really remember. On the inside, the pub was ordinary but comfortable, a few booths for privacy, candle-holders on the tables, a carpeted floor, even cushions on the chairs. There were no decorations and the music was anything but seasonal – Frank Sinatra's *In the Wee Small Hours*, one of my mother's favourites when I was a kid, playing at a low volume from concealed speakers. There were about a dozen people sitting or standing around, in ones and twos, chatting quietly or seated in silence. All but two were men. Their ages ranged from around twenty to upward of sixty. None of them looked at all familiar. No one commented on the fact that I was totally drenched and shivering with cold. I was a stranger in town and to notice me would be rude, possibly dangerous.

I went to the bar, bought a pint of Ruddles and a packet of salt and vinegar crisps, and found a seat at an unoccupied table, thankfully close to a radiator. Half an hour later, leaving my wet coat on the chair to discourage gazumping, I bought another pint. I was beginning to warm up and my soggy clothes were beginning to dry. People drifted in, some greeting various of those already present, others seemingly content to be out drinking on their own. I replenished my glass, now wholly absorbed in a sidelong study of my fellow drinkers – barflies, old friends seeking peace and quiet for a chat, some possibly clandestine lovers. These were people who wanted to be out for the evening but away from the Christmas frenzy. This was my kind of place. It was just a shame that very soon I'd have to leave it.

She was sitting opposite me before I'd even registered

her presence. 'Do you mind if I sit here?' She was maybe ten years younger than me, medium height, medium build, long dark hair that probably owed much of its gloss and hue to L'Oréal, brown eyes like polished chocolate drops. She had a glass of clear liquid with a slice of lemon and a couple of ice cubes floating on top.

'Be my guest,' I replied.

The woman took a sip of her drink. 'I've been watching you,' she said. 'You're an odd one. You look as if you belong here – but at the same time, you don't. You're not local, are you?'

'I used to be. Moved away years ago, live in London now. I'm only here today because my aunt was taken to hospital. That turned out to be a false alarm. I was on my way home to London but the line's blocked so I'm stuck here. I've been trying to work out whether I should try for a hotel or ask my cousin to put me up. Then I saw this place and thought I'd come in for a drink while I decided. It's new, isn't it?'

'Yes, it only opened a year or so ago. The owner wanted to open a place where people could go to get away from things without too much noise and crowding. That's why the music's always Sinatra, there's no happy hour or special offers, no fruit machines and no alcopops, and no seasonal themes or decorations. There's cooked food in the daytime, bar snacks in the evening. If people get loud they're asked to keep the noise down or leave. The youngsters don't come here and the big parties go elsewhere. This place is for grown-ups.'

'The owner sounds very sensible,' I said.

'I like to think so,' she said with a grin.

It was then that I realised she didn't have a coat. 'Ah,' was all I could think to say. 'Is it working out?'

'We're doing OK. A hard core of regulars has built up and they bring friends and family, plus we get a lot of passing punters looking for somewhere quiet to sit and relax. A lot of older people come here – I think it's the music. Nowhere else round here plays Sinatra round the clock. The pub doesn't make huge money but it's enough to pay the bills and give me a reasonable living.'

'The place has a nice atmosphere,' I told her. 'The cushions are a nice touch. I think it'll do well. In a way, it's so unfashionable that it'll never go out of fashion, if you know what I mean.'

'Thanks,' she said, smiling. 'That's exactly what I was aiming for.'

We talked for a while. It turned out that in some ways our lives were remarkably similar. She came from the part of London where I now lived, and had moved to my home town to take up a new job at the same age I'd been when I left it. Like me, she'd always been single; like me, there had been relationships that had never evolved into commitment. And I somehow knew that, like me, she was lonely but would never admit it.

She left the table occasionally to help out at the bar and chat with some of the regulars. *In the Wee Small Hours* became *Songs for Swingin' Lovers*, then *Frank Sinatra Sings Only for the Lonely*. But she always returned and our conversation resumed. I drank a couple more pints, relaxed, became settled. I knew I was leaving my decision until it might be too late, but I didn't care. She was good company and we were getting on like a house on fire. And I liked looking at her. I was reluctant to leave, it was as simple as that.

At around half past ten the drinkers began to drift away, back to their homes, most having now drunk just enough to be in the right frame of mind to rejoin the overblown festivities in the world outside. It was time I tried to find a berth for the night. I reached for my coat, still slightly damp, and began to say goodnight.

'Tell you what,' she said, 'why don't you stay here tonight? I have a flat upstairs. There's plenty of room.'

I was both surprised and grateful. 'Well, if you're sure,' I replied. 'That would be great, thanks. I'll have to figure out a way to get home tomorrow, though.'

'You can worry about that in the morning. But you'll have to earn your keep. If you lend a hand with the tidying-up I can let the others go home to their families sooner. Not everyone hates Christmas, you know.'

So I lent a hand, washing the tables and straightening chairs, lugging crates of empty bottles to the bins at the back of the pub. I rather enjoyed it, being part of a team engaged in light physical activity that was to a purpose. When the departing bar staff and cellarman wished us a merry Christmas, I returned the salutation, not quite as mechanically as I might usually have done.

She locked up and took me to a staircase at one side of the bar, and we went up to her flat. The contrast with the pub below was astonishing. The lounge lights were turned down very low. The cherry-wood flooring was strewn with Persian rugs; the large armchairs and sofa were upholstered in a dark green cotton fabric and augmented with soft, red cushions. The book cases were, I thought, antique mahogany, matching the drop-leaf dining table on which stood a large glass bowl filled with apples, pears and oranges. There was a small Christmas tree hung with baubles and glimmering fairy lights, and the whole flat was festooned with paper-chains, glitter and greetings cards. A non-denominational Advent calendar was pinned to the wall above a mantelpiece lined with scented candles. The flat smelled of citrus and cinnamon, nutmeg and ginger, vanilla and sandalwood, an aromatic blend so intensely sensual it made my head spin.

And it made my heart ache with longing, because this was what I'd once believed Christmas should be – intimate, magical, welcoming and enfolding, and bright with good cheer and hope for the future. This room, this display, had been put together lovingly, with care and consideration, assembled inexpensively and to wholly personal purposes. This was no grand statement of wealth, no tawdry religious sentiment, no surrender to commerce. It was, I realised, a reflection of the soul of the person who had made it. As I finally understood and appreciated what I'd been invited into, its creator was standing before me holding a short length of silvery tinsel.

'I don't have any mistletoe,' she said breathlessly as she put her warm arms around me. 'Will this do?'

That's all I remember with any clarity until I awoke in my own bed six hours ago to discover it was Boxing Day, early in the evening, and I had no memory of returning to London. There are fragments of scenes – being in her bed, eating the excellent Christmas dinner she cooked, returning to her bed, making love, the feel of her skin against mine – but it's like a jigsaw puzzle with pieces missing, a film with frames cut at random.

That's only where the conundrum begins. Four hours ago I phoned my cousin John, to find out how Aunt Rachel was doing. He was hung over and in an even worse mood than usual. According to him, there was nothing wrong with Rachel and never had been. She hadn't been taken to hospital and he hadn't sent me any e-mails saying she had. I checked my inbox and, sure enough, I couldn't find either John's e-mail or my reply saying that I was on my way. A Google search failed to find any reference to the pub I'd visited, the place I had spent two nights and a day so wonderful my memory seemed unable to retain it.

What had happened? Where had I been? As far as I could see the supplies I laid in hadn't been depleted as they should have been in those two days. The calendar hadn't been changed. Stephen King's new book was exactly as I had left it. I couldn't remember how much cash I'd had to begin with, so had no way of knowing if I really had raided it to pay for my rail ticket, but my coat was still on the rack beneath the jacket I had last worn to the office and the umbrella that would have spared me a soaking if I'd taken it with me. I hadn't been in my flat – not consciously – but it also seemed I probably hadn't been anywhere else.

The situation put me in mind of those old folktales that tell how someone is taken into the realm within a fairy mound, spending a short time there, dancing and feasting with the fairies, emerging to find many years have passed in his own world and he is only remembered as a man who went missing long ago. Or perhaps stories of abduction by aliens, in which the abductee spends hours or days with the extraterrestrials, although when they return no time has passed at all. But my experience had played out in real time. Perhaps I had merely drunk myself into a near-coma and dreamed the whole episode while I lay unconscious for nearly three days?

That would be one explanation. But it wouldn't account for the fact that my clothes, draped across the end of my bed, smelled of the perfume she wore. And it certainly would not explain the other thing, the discovery that gives me goosebumps and sends a shiver down my spine just to think of it.

In my coat pocket I found an envelope, unaddressed except for my first name, containing two items. One was a piece of tinsel about three inches in length. The other was a Christmas card. On the card someone had written a telephone number I didn't recognise and a name I now did. The area code belonged to my home town.

I'm not going to question this intrusion of magic and mystery into my life. I don't want explanations. The phone is in my hand right now. It's nearly midnight but I know she'll answer. She knows I will call.

Fatal Attractor

The nurse smiled at him as she passed. Jez Danbury nodded a cursory acknowledgement and continued setting up the equipment. She was an attractive woman with short, dark brown hair, somewhere in her late twenties, and her eyes suggested that she was interested in him. But he wasn't going there. What would be the point? If she knew anything about him, anything at all, she wouldn't want to go there either.

He glanced across the big room. Begley wasn't happy. Begley was never bloody happy. That man wouldn't know happy if it mooned at him with a big yellow smiley face painted on its arse. Danbury smiled at the unexpected mental image, just managing to suppress a laugh that would not have gone down at all well.

'What's up now, Begs?' he asked, hoping against hope that his boss wouldn't answer, knowing that Begley's frustrations would be vented in his direction.

Scowling, Begley looked up, but instead of facing Danbury he turned to his left, seemingly startled. He shook his head irritably. 'It's these readings,' he complained. 'They're all over the bloody place. Just look at this crap. It must be the new software playing up. It's the same hardware we've always used and we've never had any problems before. How the hell are we supposed to work in these bloody conditions?'

In fact, the conditions were largely of Paul Begley's own making. The man skimped on everything. He bought the cheapest hardware from the least reputable suppliers and unreliable software from unproven – and in one memorable instance, entirely bogus – companies. Value for money meant not parting with the folding stuff if humanly possible. He paid peanuts and got the monkeys *pro rata*. Jez Danbury only stayed with the firm because no one else would be likely to employ him in a position with responsibility, not with his criminal record. Although he was good at his job he knew Begley only employed him because they had been friends once, long ago, before tragedy and prison. Perhaps he'd done that out of a sense of duty. It certainly wasn't for old time's sake; Begley didn't do sentimentality. He didn't do loyalty, either. Danbury remembered a time when Begley had relentlessly pursued a girl who was already in what promised to be a lasting relationship. Yvonne had very firm views on fidelity and she had been outraged by Begley's assumption that she would cheat on her boyfriend. She had serially rebuffed Begley's advances, first politely then rudely, and reported each instance to Danbury, who had been the boyfriend in question. The situation had severely tested his friendship with the man who was now his employer.

But that had been before. Now there was no Yvonne and friendship too had gone.

'Let me take a look,' Danbury suggested. 'Might be

able to spot where the problem is from the read-out.'

Begley stared at him. He seemed to be internally debating Danbury's worth as a trouble-shooter, which Danbury found intensely annoying, as that was exactly what he was paid to do. Today he was only out in the field because they were so thinly stretched, but he had the necessary skills to set up the equipment and interpret the readings. Indeed, his expertise was far greater than that of anyone else in the firm. It didn't count for much.

Eventually Begley reluctantly handed over the sheaf of papers. Danbury scrutinised them and frowned. 'Begs, there's nothing wrong with these readings. Yeah, they're a bit high but isn't that what we're supposed to be looking for?'

'Well, yes – but we're not supposed to be actually finding anything.'

Danbury was puzzled. 'Well, if we're not supposed to find anything – Begs, what the bloody hell are we doing here?'

The firm's remit was defined with some precision in its literature and internal memos: To detect and eliminate electro-magnetic anomalies affecting or potentially affecting IT, customers or the human components of corporate machinery. This meant anything that could foul up wi-fi or mobile phone connectivity, screw up networked computer systems or pose a threat to health. The recent flood of health-scare stories in the newspapers and on television had resulted in a public panic and a financial boom for Electro-Magnetic Pathology Services – EM-PathS – but Begley had responded in his usual way, refusing to invest or increase operational budgets. Consequently their resources, human and material, were spread thinly and at present not even up to the normal poor standards. Danbury reckoned only lack of meaningful competition stood between EM-PathS and the Official Receiver; between himself and the local Jobcentre.

'I don't understand. Why are we here if we're not supposed to find anything?'

'That's exactly my point,' Begley patiently explained. 'We're here to give this place a clean bill of health. They pay us and we piss off to do another place. They're reassured, their customers are relieved and we make money. Everyone's happy. What we do not do is tell them they have a problem that might prove expensive or even impossible to fix.'

Danbury was sceptical. He didn't believe the recent health scares. He'd worked with IT, microwave, radio and electrical equipment all his life – except of course for those seven years in the penal system – and been exposed to some pretty serious electro-magnetism. As far as he was aware it hadn't affected his health at all. He felt fit and well, and had passed his regular medical check-ups with flying colours, or so he'd been told. All that crap about mobile phones and power-lines causing cancer – well, crap was exactly what it was. As for electro-magnetism, he'd heard all about Michael Persinger's work on inducing religious or mystical, even shamanic, experiences using electro-magnetic stimulation of the brain, but it was clear from Persinger's results that the phenomenon only lasted as long as the stimulation and had no adverse effects in the long-term. In fact, Danbury was slightly resentful that in his career he had never been affected in that way. He'd always wanted to experience something profound and otherworldly, even though he didn't really believe in that sort of thing. It might give his life the meaning it now so sorely lacked.

He gazed at his surroundings – an Accident and Emergency admissions area in a well-known London hospital – and wondered what could be causing the high readings. It was probably malfunctioning equipment. Nowadays every medical facility was a temple to digital technology, which kept EM output much lower than the old days of valves and cathode ray tubes. But there were some devices – X-ray machines, defibrillators, MRI and CAT scanners – that pumped out a fair amount of electromagnetism or microwave radiation. He couldn't see anything like that in the vicinity. He did feel oddly content, though – vaguely optimistic and almost euphoric. That was as unexpected as the humorous thought he had experienced only minutes earlier.

'Tell you what, Begs,' he said. 'Let's see if we can isolate the source. It's probably an old television set or computer monitor that they couldn't be bothered to upgrade and now it's playing up. Think about it – if we actually find something every now and again it'll be good for business. If we keep finding nothing someone's going to take the logical next step and assume that what we do is a waste of time and money.'

Begley thought about it. Yes, that made sense. Maybe Danbury was worth his salary after all and was not just a charity case, the millstone around his neck. 'OK,' he grudgingly allowed. 'But I'm off to grab some lunch. I could murder a pie and chips. And for Christ's sake don't let the staff here know anything's up. You know what people are like. They talk. Be discreet and find me a tiny little gremlin that we can give them to stamp on.'

When Begley had gone, Danbury restarted the scans and took readings from a variety of locations within the waiting area, hoping to be able to locate the source of the anomalous electro-magnetism by triangulation. The additional work would mean a late return home but that was fine by him – he had no reason to rush back to his lonely, depressing little flat. Keeping busy always suited him. Although stoical by nature, he constantly needed tasks to occupy his mind, to stop him thinking about what he had done – and what he had endured and deserved. Inactivity was the last thing he wanted. Besides, he liked the atmosphere in this place. It was oddly soothing, even comforting. It had been a long time since he had felt either of those things.

The nurses and doctors and porters smiled cheerfully at him as he went about his business. Danbury hadn't noticed that. Everyone there seemed happy in their work. Even the patients were happy. The nice-looking nurse who had smiled at him before did so as she passed him again, and he nodded once more but this time didn't make eye-contact. He didn't want to risk encouraging her. He shrugged to himself and set up the instruments in a new spot.

Typically, Begley took a long lunch, seemingly oblivious to the possibility that Danbury might need a break himself. When he returned, three hours later, Danbury was standing outside the entrance to A&E, smoking a cigarette and drinking machine-made coffee from a flimsy white plastic cup. He appeared to be deep in thought.

'You found it then.' Begley assumed that if his subordinate had stopped working then the problem must be sorted. 'Come on, don't stand around. Let's get that equipment in the van and go to the next job.'

Danbury didn't reply. He continued to smoke and sip coffee. Begley realised that Danbury wasn't looking at him but through him. The man's gaze was fixed at a point a long way behind his boss.

'Danbury? What's the matter with you?'

'I couldn't locate the source,' said Danbury absently. 'There is no source, Begs. The EM is all around that waiting area.'

'Well, it must be coming from somewhere, surely?'

'Yeah, obviously it's coming from somewhere. But I can't find a source.'

'Sorted then – if there's no source it stands to reason that there's no problem. Danbury? Hello? Are you with us or away with the bloody fairies? What's up?'

Danbury pulled himself together and lit another cigarette. 'This is where they brought us that night.'

'Sorry, you've lost me. What night do you mean?'

'You know, the night of your party. This is the first time I've been back here.'

It was so fresh in Danbury's memory that it might have been only days ago, not nearly ten years in the past. The party, the girl he'd been going out with for a few months. Dancing and laughing. Then a jumbled blur of shouting and sirens and flashing blue lights, waking up to questions, accusations and the revelation of horror. The police had pieced it all together and the Crown Prosecution Service had applied the glue that fixed it in place. Yvonne had been given a dose of heroin, not enough to kill but sufficient to incapacitate, and had then been raped and savagely beaten. And he, Jez Danbury, had done it. True, he had no memory of actually doing it – but it had been his semen inside the girl and he alone had been with her in that locked bedroom when they'd broken down the door. Her blood had been on his hands. He didn't recall buying the smack, taking the drug himself or injecting it into Yvonne. They often smoked a bit of weed, sure – but they'd never touched anything harder. He didn't know why he had raped her when they had made love only that afternoon, less than two hours before the party. Perhaps the heroin had affected him badly. He had no memory of it. But it could have been no one else. The facts spoke for themselves.

Yvonne had died in that very admissions area and he had spent seven years in prison for her rape and murder. The rape had been assumed by the police and CPS simply because they could discover no other motive. Danbury had only briefly considered that particular accusation might be unjust but it paled beside the greater charge. Unable to dispute the evidence for that, he had pleaded guilty on all counts. The trial had been a formality. Haunted by grief and guilt, Danbury had meekly accepted the sentence. If any other man had killed Yvonne he would have thirsted for the death penalty that no longer existed. As it was, he thought it far too lenient. When other inmates came for him in the night and used him in the same way he had used Yvonne, he accepted that too. He deserved the humiliation and pain for snuffing out that precious life, the life of a girl he had come to love. No punishment could be too severe. It was a debt he could never repay.

'That was a long time ago,' Begley told him. 'It was a bad night and we were all out of our minds on drugs. At least you didn't have to explain to my parents why our house was crawling with the Old Bill. My old man went potty when they got home. I got a right earful.'

Good old Begley. His minor troubles were always so much worse than other people's major disasters. Danbury didn't mind. He was still feeling oddly relaxed and at peace. He was distracted, daydreaming. The guilt was still there but for the first time in years it was taking a back seat to something else, a kind of yearning.

'She was only eighteen, Begs.'

'Yes, and we were only nineteen. And at least I had a job ready and waiting for you when you got out.'

'I can't imagine how I could have done it. I know the evidence was solid, but I honestly can't imagine. I was in love with her, Begs. We were talking about getting engaged. I'd never have hurt her. I wouldn't have hurt anyone. Why did I do it?'

Begley sighed and shook his head grumpily. 'Forget about it, it's done and dusted. It was ten bloody years ago. I thought you were past harping on about it. God, you're giving me the creeps.' It was as sympathetic as he got. 'Come on, let's go in and check those readings again.'

They set up the instruments again and took new readings. As Danbury said, it proved impossible to isolate a source. Begley had a quick look round for malfunctioning electronics but found nothing. The area of unusually high electro-magnetism was almost perfectly circular, encompassing the entire admissions area and parts of several corridors leading off it. There was no gradual reduction in strength – inside that circle the field was strong and consistent; outside the boundary it fell sharply to almost nothing.

Begley was looking over to the admissions desk, frowning.

'You OK, Begs?'

'Yes – just I saw someone I thought I recognised, a woman over by that sign that says "triage", but there's no one there. I only saw her out of the corner of my eye. I must be seeing things. That's what happens when you have too much work and not enough sleep.'

'No, all I can see is a couple of blokes in overalls loafing around, and there's a paramedic just outside the door having a fag. It must be a slow day.'

Danbury looked closely at Begley. His boss and former friend seemed unnerved, apparently watching and listening for something. The man started suddenly and looked over his shoulder, then to his left. Danbury stared at him, unable to work out why the man was so edgy. Couldn't he feel how calm and peaceful this place was? He sighed and returned his attention to the instruments.

'There's something wrong here, Begs. The amount of EM we're picking up can't be from ordinary medical or IT gear. An old TV set wouldn't do it. A bloody generator wouldn't explain these readings. It's much too powerful.'

Begley was looking over at the admissions desk again, his face now expressing something like alarm. 'Did you see her?' he asked.

'See who?' Danbury was at a loss. It wasn't like Begley to be so jumpy. His normal response to any irritant was scowling and harsh language, never nervousness. But Begley had the look of a man at the end of his tether, and for no apparent reason. Danbury, on the other hand, was beginning to feel euphoric again, and that wasn't like him at all. They were both behaving in an uncharacteristic fashion.

'Never mind,' muttered Begley.

When Danbury went to dismantle one set of instruments so they could be moved to another point within the circle, he was surprised to see a little old lady in a pink dressing gown watching him, a beatific expression on her wrinkled face.

'Such a pretty child,' she told him.

'Sorry,' he smiled politely. 'I don't know who you mean.'

'The girl,' the old lady told him. 'She's looking at you, boy. She's happy to see you. I come here to see my Mark. He died here, just like she must have done. This is a happy place. Look at all the nurses, all of them smiling. They feel it, sometimes they see it.'

Danbury drew the obvious conclusion, that the woman was a refugee from the psychiatric ward. Nevertheless, he was curious. 'What do you see, exactly?'

'Oh, mostly it's just like shadows flitting by and I can't get a good look at them. Sometimes I see them quite clearly, like my Mark. They're all happy because they know the people here tried their best to save them. It means a lot to them. That girl, she's still looking at you. She's got red hair and she's wearing a pale blue dress. There's a silver charm bracelet on her left wrist and a watch on her right. She's trying to speak to you but I can't hear her. I can't hear any of them. I just see.'

Danbury froze, astonished. Yvonne was blonde but

had coloured her hair copper-red only a couple of days before the party. She was left-handed so wore watches on her right wrist. The bracelet had been a sixteenth birthday present from her mother. She had worn a light blue dress that night. Danbury's mouth was suddenly dry and his scalp was tingling. His heart began to pound.

'You say she's smiling at me?'

'Yes, a big smile. But not when she looks at that other man, him over there.' She pointed at Begley, who was cursing under his breath as he tried to study yet another set of unacceptably high readings while still restlessly casting his eyes around the room.

'No, she doesn't like him at all.'

The woman walked slowly away, shaking her head, pausing only briefly to beam a smile toward a point in the room where no one was.

Danbury was unsettled. The old woman had described Yvonne as she had been the night she died. How was that possible? The half-glimpsed shadowy entities fitted in with what he knew of Persinger's experiments with electromagnetic stimulation of the brain. There should be other sensations – piercing and perceived disappearance of body parts, like the discomforts associated with alien abduction, shamanic initiation and the torments of Hell – but he had never heard of subjects seeing real, long dead people they could never have known. And he had never heard of anyone experiencing such effects without Persinger's specialist equipment, the so-called 'God helmet' that allowed different parts of the brain to be stimulated.

Begley was looking at that empty spot by the admissions desk again. This time he was looking very scared.

'Jez, are you sure you can't see her?'

'See who, Begs? Where?'

'Over there,' Begley pointed a trembling finger. 'She looks just like that girl, you were going out with, the one that you – the one that died. Yvonne. She keeps looking at me. She looks bloody furious. Oh shit – what's happened to my leg? Jez, my right leg's gone!'

Danbury looked down at the magnetometer he had been monitoring, just in time to see the reading go off the scale, so fast that the motion made him jump. Small metal objects flew from tables and work surfaces and hit the floor; a trolley sped past him, apparently of its own volition. Begley screamed that his arms had vanished then fell to the floor, whining that little grey men were pushing long needles into his body. Danbury was as frustrated as he was alarmed. He could see nothing, only Begley in the throes of some kind of seizure. A doctor and two nurses ran over to Begley, who was now writhing in apparent agony and screaming in terror.

After a few minutes, Begley became calm and sat up. He looked sick and old, his eyes haunted. A nurse, the pretty brunette who had smiled at Danbury, was asking Begley questions about his health and any medication he might be taking but he wasn't paying her any attention.

'Begs, are you OK?' Danbury asked. He didn't understand what was happening.

Begley gave a nervous laugh and a sickly grin. 'I'm going to Hell, Jez. That was a little foretaste. That's what it will be like for me forever.'

'You're not making any sense, Begs. Going to Hell?

Why?'

'You didn't see her, did you?' Begley laughed again, this time an unpleasant, cracked sound. 'She was right there beside me while they were doing those things to me just now. Her face – I could tell from her face that it wouldn't stop until I did what she wanted. They'd keep tormenting me until I told you that it was me. That night, it was me.'

Danbury still couldn't quite grasp what Begley was saying. 'You've lost me, mate. I haven't the faintest idea what you're talking about.'

'Someone spiked your drink and you went into my parents' bedroom to lie down,' said Begley, his voice quiet and tremulous. 'When Yvonne went to see if you were OK, you were out cold. I was already in there, about to shoot up a little smack. I'd taken a bit too much speed and needed something to take the edge off, but when she came in all I could think off was getting her in bed. You know how much I fancied her. I'd fancied her for ages, ever since you first met her. I was bloody obsessed with her. I tried to talk her into having sex with me but she told me to piss off. I got angry and I hit her. I hit her a few times and then I...'

The nurse at Begley's side stood and stared stonily down at him, her face set and her eyes serious. Begley avoided her eyes and Danbury's. He stared at the floor, the only place left that was safe to look at.

'Jez, I don't know how to say this. But I've got to. I've got to confess. I saw it in Yvonne's face. It's the only way. She was unconscious. I was going to – you know. But I couldn't do it, not after that. I knew she was badly hurt and I was too bloody scared. Then I panicked, shot you both up with a bit of smack to keep you quiet while I tried to figure out what to do next. I wasn't thinking straight. But she woke up while I was injecting her and started screaming, so I hit her again, very hard, and wiped some of the blood onto your hands. I hid behind the door while the others kicked it in. They didn't see that I was already there so I just joined the crowd and pretended I'd come in with them.'

The nurse looked questioningly at Danbury, but his horrified eyes were fixed on Begley. Then she walked angrily to the entrance, fumbling in her pocket for a mobile phone.

'You killed Yvonne,' said Danbury eventually, torn between rage and despair but somehow maintaining stillness and a sombre dignity. 'You beat her and killed her. And all these years you let me believe I'd done it, you rotten bastard. You let me suffer all that guilt. I spent seven years inside for what you did. I was raped myself in the prison, Begs, at least a dozen times. I didn't care about that then because I thought it was what I deserved, another part of my punishment. But I fucking care about it now and I hate you for what you did to her. That was just fucking despicable.'

'I know,' replied Begley quietly. 'It's why despite giving you this job I've never been able to bring myself to treat you well, to be your friend again. If I had it would have meant admitting my own guilt, acknowledging what I was and what I'd done. Sometimes I almost believed it really was you that killed her. But now I know what's coming to me it doesn't matter anymore. She was just giving me a little taste of what forever holds for me. I'm going to Hell, Jez. I deserve it. Maybe I'm there already. But maybe if I confess now it would stand in my favour when I'm judged.'

Danbury was disgusted. Even after admitting what he had done, Begley was still thinking primarily of himself. He hadn't even expressed contrition, either for the murder or what Danbury had suffered in the intervening years. If there really was a Hell, Danbury didn't think a confession made for the wrong reasons would cut any ice with God or the Devil. He certainly hoped it wouldn't and that Old Nick's lads had a plentiful supply of pitchforks and red-hot pokers. For a moment he was tempted to pre-empt divine judgement and beat Begley to a pulp. But he was curiously unable to act on the impulse. The rage washed over him in waves but vanished to leave only a dull sadness. It was, he decided, the strangely relaxing effect the room was having on him. It had rendered him inert. Anyway, he decided, with any luck the hypothetical red-hot pokers destined for Begley would be foreshadowed by the very real attentions of people like those who had abused Danbury when he was inside. It would be a kind of justice.

After that, Danbury had nothing further to say to Begley or anyone else present. He became a mere spectator as the drama came to its conclusion. Summoned by the nurse, two burly security guards came to ensure Begley stayed put. After a while, the police arrived, taking names and addresses of the witnesses and trying to make a coherent narrative of what had happened. Begley merely told them that he wished to confess to a murder and was led off, leaving Danbury standing alone, still numbed by what had just taken place.

Danbury walked over to the empty spot by the admissions desk. He stood there for a few minutes, trying to open himself up to any lingering presence. But if there was anything there he couldn't feel it or see it. He couldn't make contact. His guilt, an enormous burden he had carried for nearly a decade, had vanished with Begley's revelation but he felt incredibly tired and anything but liberated. He sighed wearily. All he wanted now was to say goodbye to the girl he had loved and thought he had killed, but he could find no one to bid farewell. But at least he could say the words and hope they would be heard.

'Goodbye Yvonne,' he whispered to the empty space. 'See you later, maybe.'

Before he was halfway to the exit the pretty nurse reappeared. She had a coat on over her uniform.

'Hi,' she said. 'I was wondering if you were OK. I couldn't believe what that man said. What he did to that girl was just terrible and so was what he did to you. What kind of bastard could do something like that? Look, I've just finished my shift. My name's Lynne. Do you fancy coming for a drink?'

Danbury tried unsuccessfully to cover his surprise. Since his release from prison hadn't even considered going out with another woman. At first he had mourned Yvonne. Then he simply hadn't bothered. Those who knew about his past would never have gone out with him – and with his small social world it was a fair bet that any woman he was likely to meet would know all about him in advance. Why should any woman trust him when he didn't trust himself? Now, for the first time in years, he wondered if perhaps a real life was possible after all. Maybe that had been why Yvonne had made Begley confess to him, to free him from the chains of the past so that he could begin again, so that he could find happiness once more. Why not take this unforeseen opportunity? He smiled uncertainly at the nurse. She returned the smile. She was forthright and decisive, a strong woman. A woman who knew what she wanted. Danbury liked that, just as he had liked it about Yvonne. And yes, Lynne was very attractive.

'Sure,' he replied. 'That would be nice, Lynne. Perhaps we could have dinner as well. You can help me spend the last of my money. After this I think I can wave goodbye to my job. I expect a redundancy payment will also be out of the question. I'm Jez – that's short for Jeremiah, believe it or not. My parents are a bit old-fashioned. Not that I've spoken to them in a long time. They're probably even more old-fashioned by now.'

'What about all that equipment? Are you going to just leave it there?'

Danbury thought about it for less than a second. 'What about it? It doesn't belong to me and I don't think Begley's going to be needing it anymore.'

He offered her his arm and she took it, laughing with delight at the gallant gesture. Out of the corner of his eye he caught a sudden flash of red hair and a shimmer of blue. There was a prolonged clangour as basins, medical instruments and other objects flew through the air and struck metal surfaces, seemingly at random. The exit doors slammed shut. Every exposed part of Danbury's skin itched and his hair stood on end. Something that felt like a long, sharp pin seemed to prick his abdomen. Then another pierced his chest and sent his heart into spasm.

Lynne screamed as her legs buckled beneath her and she fell to the floor.

Nobody Special

I opened one eye and tried to focus. The glowing blue digits said it was twenty minutes to three in the morning. That was bad enough. Then I registered what she'd just said. 'But it isn't due for another three weeks.'

Somewhere in the back of my mind I was aware that these things couldn't be calculated down to the exact minute, not even to the day. There would always be a grey area, the one between last known menstruation and sexual intercourse. And who keeps a record of every time they've made love with their partner? Yes, I know there are some people who obsess about things like that, but not us. Well, certainly not this half of us. OK, I keep a record, on an Excel spreadsheet, of United's results, with dates, half-time scores, goal scorers, red and yellow cards, the teams and substitutions, percentage of possession, shots on and off target, corners, fouls – and I manipulate these with formulae, data filters, all the analytical tools at my disposal. But it's just a harmless hobby. Does a person's sex life count as one of those? Come to think of it, I suppose that for some people it does. But not in this household. Definitely not.

I was procrastinating and I knew it. The fact was that I'd had a late night – yes, I'd been up producing a pie chart of United's average scoring times, broken down into five-minute match segments – and it was still only two-forty in the morning. I was tired, warm, comfortable, snug… And there was something else at the back of my drifting mind, but that could wait until…

'Don't go back to bloody sleep,' she said crossly. 'It's happening now. My waters have broken and I'm sure that pain in my belly isn't down to last night's vindaloo. Get your useless fat arse out of bed and get dressed. We're going to the hospital. Right now.'

Fat arse? She was a fine one to talk, though to be fair that was down to gravidity. Admittedly, in my case a spot of middle-age spread had set in recently, but that was mostly down to my sportingly joining in with her food cravings and 'eating for two' – alright, a notional four – in the manner nowadays expected of a modern, sensitive non-female life-partner of the heterosexual persuasion. No one could say I hadn't embraced our pregnancy. I'd even gone along to ante-natal classes, done the exercises with her, learned how to breathe properly and worn the fake pregnant belly so that I would have an appreciation of what it means to be carting a spare human being around with you, albeit a miniature one. I now knew how to change nappies, deal with infant vomit and initiate the expulsion of wind. I was a fully-trained male parent, fit and ready for twenty-first century fatherhood.

What was she complaining about? OK, so I still hadn't fixed those shelves that had fallen down, and the promised hand-made crib was yet to escape the drawing-board, but I could cook, clean and utter sympathetic cooing noises as well as any woman I knew. I'd certainly done my domestic bit before tailing off the previous evening with a relaxing forensic examination of United's recent, unremarkable form. The potatoes were peeled, cut and ready for roasting. Pigs were wrapped tightly in blankets. The turkey was roasting serenely in a slow oven. The pudding was primed, and there would be home-made brandy butter. The presents were wrapped, tagged and beribboned. And that was what had been in the back of my mind. It was Christmas morning.

I sat bolt upright. 'But it's Christmas,' I pointed out. 'You can't give birth before we've had dinner.'

She glared at me. 'Want to bet on that? Get dressed and try to remember where you left the car keys.'

Reluctantly, I rose and began hunting for my trousers, by coincidence the last known location of the keys. She could read me like a book. 'They're in the laundry basket,' she said as she sat at the dressing table and started applying cosmetics. 'Anyway, you need a shower first. You're not coming with me smelling like that.'

'Like what?'

'Like you've just crawled out of bed.'

'I *have* just crawled out of bed. Under protest, I might add. And why are you putting on make-up? You're having a baby, not going to a dinner and dance.'

'I want to look my best when I welcome our firstborn. She won't want to see her mother looking like something just dug up from the local graveyard. And it won't do to have her father stinking like one. Go on, shower.'

'Should I shave as well?'

'No. You'll look more of a manly role model if you don't. The child might even be able to forgive that flabby belly of yours.'

I was about to point out that her bulging midriff put mine to shame, but thought better of it. After all, I could be blamed for that, too. And no doubt would be, in the years to come. But perhaps not today. Today meant peace on earth, joy and glad tidings, and goodwill to all men. Even me, surely?

'Can I open my presents before we go?'

Well, maybe not all men. I hurried to the bathroom as the shouting and cursing began.

Halfway to the hospital, the lights went out. She'd been grumbling and swearing all the way, mostly about and at me. I was gasping for a fag and a mug of strong coffee, not being given time for either before being nagged out of the front door and into the car. Smoking was, of course, strictly *verboten* in her presence, a state of affairs that long pre-dated her pregnancy. I was hoping against hope that I'd get an opportunity to slip out for a crafty drag while the maternity unit staff prepped her for parturition – with any luck the hospital cafeteria would be open and I could also get some breakfast. But my dreams of sustenance were derailed by the world outside the car suddenly going dark. Street lighting, shop windows, traffic lights, gaudy Christmas decorations – everything winked out, leaving only the headlights to show where we were going. Then the engine died and they too failed.

'What the hell have you done now?' she complained.

'It wasn't me,' I replied, trying to guide the slowing vehicle into the kerb. 'I think it's a power cut. I don't know what's wrong with the car – I filled the tank yesterday and the battery should be OK.'

The car halted and I applied the handbrake. I pressed the switch on the interior light but nothing happened. The only lights I could see anywhere were very faint, up in the sky, and a very long way away.

'Right,' she said, folding her arms. 'Phone for a taxi.'

I took the mobile phone from my shirt pocket and pressed the speed-dial icon for the local taxi firm. There was no dialling tone. I tried again.

'No signal,' I said.

'Bloody typical,' she growled. 'I told you to keep that thing charged, just in case. Why don't you ever listen?'

'Look,' I said wearily, 'it's fully charged. But there's no signal. The network must be down. Shit, we're going to have to walk there.'

'I can't walk all that way in this condition,' she said. 'I'm getting contractions. I don't want to give birth in the gutter. You'll have to carry me.'

'Carry you?' I was aghast. 'I'd never make it. Look at the size of you.'

Her eyes narrowed dangerously. 'Are you saying I'm fat?'

'No, just that there are two of you and one's wrapped in a lot of heavy packaging.'

'You could give me a piggy-back.'

'No bloody way. We'll have to get out and see if we can thumb a lift.'

'Don't be an ass. Have you seen anyone else on the

road since we started out? Anyone at all? It's a quarter to four on Christmas morning. Everyone's in bed. Even the emergency services won't have much to do. We're on our own out here. On our own. And I need the toilet.'

She put her face in her hands and began to cry.

By the time we reached the hospital I was knackered, completely out of breath, and soaked in perspiration. My knees and arms ached abominably. And she'd peed down my back. The weather was worsening – it was freezing cold and thick snow was falling. Very Christmassy, but the very last thing I needed. I wanted to know how it was it possible to be hot and sweaty and suffering from hypothermia at the same time. Fortunately, my face and body had shielded my wife from the worst of the bitterly cold wind and deflected most of the snow. That was no great comfort.

At least the hospital's emergency power supply was working. The lights were dimmer than I'd have expected but A&E was blessedly warm and cosy, trimmed with festive tinsel and paper chains. There was even a decorated tree with twinkly fairy lights. Except for us, the plastic angel on top of the tree, and a solitary receptionist, the place was empty. I deposited my burden in the waiting area and went to the desk.

'I'm sorry,' the receptionist said. 'The maternity unit is full.'

'Full? What do you mean, full?'

'Well, technically I suppose it isn't. But we had to close half the beds. Cuts. You'll have to go to St James', across town. They've probably still got some beds free.'

'We can't. My car's broken down, there's no public

transport, and there's a blizzard blowing out there.'

'You could phone for a cab.'

I sighed, pulled out my phone and dialled the taxi firm again. 'No signal. See?'

She pointed. 'There's a land line over there. It's free, connects directly with Jack's Taxis.'

I walked across to the phone, picked up the receiver and pressed the button to connect me. After a minute of silence I memorised the number and returned to the desk. 'No connection. It's dead. Maybe I could use your phone?'

Reluctantly, she gestured for me to go round to her side of the desk. I dialled Jack's Taxis. 'Nothing,' I said after a while. Then I dialled our usual taxi number. 'Still nothing.' As an afterthought I punched in our home telephone number. 'The phones must be down completely,' I said, when that too brought only silence. 'Look here, my wife's waters have broken, she's having contractions, and she's in no fit state to go anywhere. This is a bloody hospital, for Christ's sake. Bugger the cuts. You must be able to do *something.*'

The receptionist tutted and rolled her eyes, then stood and walked across to one in a row of curtained alcoves, where she exchanged a few words with what appeared to be a corpse on a gurney. The dead man levered himself into a sitting position, yawned and rubbed his eyes. 'I'll be right with you,' he called. 'Sonya, can you get me a coffee while I sort this?'

'Make it two coffees,' I suggested. Sonya gave me a look that could have freeze-dried an erupting volcano, then strode off.

The ex-corpse ambled across to me, yawning again.

His clothes were rumpled, his eyes were red-rimmed and he badly needed a shave. He had my sympathy, though I was pretty confident that no one had pissed down his back. 'Sorry about that,' he said. 'We told Sonya not to disturb us. She can take things a bit literally. What's the trouble?'

'My wife's about to give birth. The receptionist said the maternity unit has no spare beds, but we can't get anywhere else – the phones are out, there's a power cut, and there's a snowstorm outside.'

'That's right, we're supposed to redirect maternity cases to St James'. It's the cuts. And we're short staffed as it is, what with the flu that's going round. Only five of us here on the front line, plus Sonya, to deal with all these patients.'

I looked around us. 'But there's no one here except us. You were having a kip. You're not actually doing anything.'

'Yeah, but we could be. If there was a major incident we'd be right up shit creek, wouldn't we?' He stifled another yawn. 'Where's Sonya got to with that bloody coffee? Hey, I don't suppose you've got a fag on you?'

After swilling back a large mug of coffee and cadging two of my roll-ups, the junior doctor – John something, I didn't catch the surname – wandered into the bowels of the hospital, returning twenty minutes later with another doctor and a young nurse. There was something furtive about the new medic, who didn't bother introducing himself, while the nurse appeared vaguely embarrassed. I wondered if they'd been up to mischief in one of the other cubicles.

Whatever, they were bound to have been having more fun than I was. My wife's groans were escalating in volume and escaping with increasing frequency. While Doctor John had been outside smoking my ciggies I'd been ordered to remain inside and tend to my spouse. Sonya the receptionist gave her a cup of tea and received a sweet smile of gratitude. I got nothing but a prolonged glare and silent blame for – well, just about everything.

The assembled team manoeuvred the expectant mother into a cubicle and onto a trolley, which had been kitted out in a fair approximation of a bed. They did medical things and acted professionally. I stood around uselessly and generally got in the way. But otherwise it went very smoothly and remarkably quickly. So I was there when our first-born made his entrance – which was a bit of a surprise, as we'd been told he would be a girl – and didn't pass out once, not even at the messiest parts of the proceedings. The doctors fussed over my wife while the nurse scurried off with the kid and brought him back bathed, wrapped in a sky-blue blanket, and with a tag fastened around one ankle. The tag had a slot for a slip of card. The nurse produced a ballpoint pen from one of her uniform pockets and looked helplessly at me.

'Do you have a name for him yet?'

'We'd decided on Melanie,' I said. 'But that's probably out now.'

'Joshua,' my wife snapped. 'That's my father's name. We'll call him Joshua. We can sort out a middle name before we register the birth.'

'Right,' replied the nurse. 'Joshua Carpenter it is. Here you go.'

She handed the baby to my wife, who smiled stupidly, stroked his sparse hair, cooed for a few minutes, then held him out to me. 'Here, you hold him. Hold little Josh.'

Knowing what was good for me, I did as she said. I was terrified – afraid that I might drop him, squeeze him too hard, obstruct his airways, all the fears and dreads a new father might experience when dealing with a fragile newborn. Then I began to feel something else. Suspicion.

'He's got blue eyes,' I observed. 'Ours are brown.'

'They all have blue eyes at first,' the nameless doctor told me, rather impatiently.

'Yeah, but these are really blue. And he's blond.'

'That often happens. It will darken with time.'

'What about that nose? It's completely different to mine – or yours, Miriam. Ours are – well, mine is quite prominent. He's got a button-nose, tiny. And those ears are a bit, um, pointy.'

There was a short, tense silence, then my wife spoke. 'What are you *saying*, Joe?'

I knew that tone. I knew that look. It meant serious trouble. 'Nothing,' I said hastily. 'Nothing at all. As the doctor said, he'll probably grow into them. Or they'll grow into him. Whatever.' I tickled the child's chin. 'Look, he's got my – er – fingers. A regular chip off the old block, eh? Hi, little Josh. Say hello to your old man.'

They found Miriam a bed in a private room just off the children's ward, bright pink and blue walls, lots of stuffed toy animals. Just the thing for a five year-old. They got her settled in while I hurried back to the car – 'hurried' is perhaps putting it a bit strongly; I trudged as fast as I could through deepening snow, straining against a howling, icy wind – to collect her overnight bag, which we'd been forced to leave behind on the way there. God knows what was in it. It weighed nearly as much as she did in her pre-partum state. My car, miraculously, started first time, so at least the return journey was less debilitating, even if on a normal day I could have walked faster than I was able to drive in those conditions.

By the time I got back, the power supply had been restored. The street lights went on, shop windows blazed into life, my phone started buzzing to announce the arrival of text messages and e-mails – perhaps festive greetings from friends abroad or local early risers, but more likely a flood of advertising for the post-Yule, pre-New Year sales. We may rest but Mammon rarely takes a breather.

There was a bit of a commotion at the hospital entrance. A small mob of people, some dressed as elves, a few Puffa-jacketed, doughy-featured men with cameras, good-natured shouts and flash photography. Somehow, a security guard had managed to put in an appearance – I guessed he'd been snoozing in one of the cubicles when I'd been desperate for assistance – so I asked him what was going on.

'That bloke from *I'm A Celebrity*,' he said, shivering with cold but perfectly happy to die of hypothermia if it meant basking in a little reflected starlight. 'You know, the one who was shagging that Samantha what's-her-name off that soap before she came out as a lesbian. He's turned up dressed as Father Christmas, sack of presents for the kids, bunch of photographers in tow. Look, he autographed my time-sheet. Diamond geezer.'

I peered at the scrawl but was unable to decipher it. Bruce? Bruno? Brendan? Brian? Brrrrr-it's-bloody-cold? There was no one around in a Father Christmas outfit so even if I'd known who the guard was talking about I couldn't even try to identify him. I shrugged and pushed my way through the throng. It was none of my business and I was not at all interested in celebrities I'd never heard of. Though I did wonder what the security firm's payroll staff would make of that signature when the guard tried to claim his dosh.

When I got back to the children's ward, pandemonium was in full swing. Kids were squealing and whooping, running, hobbling, and in one case, crawling around a tall man dressed in bright red and brilliant white who was dishing out gaily-wrapped packages and boxes of sweets and yelling what might have been 'Ho, ho, ho,' if the enormous false beard hadn't muffled it.

In the room where my wife and child lay, I found three alarmingly thin but unfeasibly large-breasted young women in elf costumes and the kind of eyelashes and hair extensions you need planning permission for. They were gathered around the bed, twittering animatedly at each other and Miriam in grating Essex accents, admiring my son Josh.

'Ooh, look – isn't he gorgeous? I wish my eyes were that blue.'

'Leave it out Shazza, yours are hazel. Cassie's are nearly that shade, though. I wouldn't mind a dress that colour. What's his name? Josh? That's nice. I went out with a bloke called Josh once. He dumped me for my friend's brother.'

'Come on, Mel. It's my turn to hold him. Oh bless – he's giving me a little smile. Where's his dad? Still at home in bed, I'll bet. Men. They're all the same. Look at the job we had getting Barry up this morning. And he was still pissed from last night.'

'Yeah, and we had to kick that little slapper out of his bed. Honestly, fame's gone right to his head.'

'Huh, you're telling me. Barry bloody Gabriel, the Big I Am. What a twat. If this PA job didn't pay so well, I'd have been on my bike weeks ago.'

'Was it a girl, though? I thought she might be a lady-boy. Not that Barry was sober enough to care. Anyway, the thick bastard probably wouldn't have twigged even if he hadn't been rat-arsed.'

'Whatever she was, rather her than me.'

I cleared my throat loudly and clumped noisily into the room, but I might as well have been the invisible man in a home for the profoundly deaf. Wholly ignored, I dumped the bag by the bed and collapsed into a chair half-occupied by a giant teddy bear whose expression was as weary and uncomprehending as my own. I took the opportunity to doze. Meanwhile, the buxom elves maintained their bird-like chatter.

After a while, I became dimly aware that they had broken out the cosmetics and toiletries and were giving Miriam an in-bed make-over. One was testing perfumes on her wrists. Another was applying spangled gold nail varnish. The third was offering some sort of balm she said was guaranteed to get her back on her feet in no time. I watched and listened in bleary horror for a few minutes, then zoned out.

But I was not destined to rest. The door burst open and in walked Father Christmas. I couldn't help but notice that he was a bit unsteady on his pins, and he reeked of whisky. Swaying, he began to sing, and not very well.

'Silent night, holy night!
All is calm, all is bright.
Round yon Virgin, Mother and Child.
Holy infant so tender and mild,
Sleep in heavenly peace,
Sleep in heavenly peace.'

Fat chance of that with all that racket and fuss going on around me. Barry Gabriel, the man famous only for being famous and hanging out with famous people – Barry Gabriel, the Big I Am – continued to sing and clown around and exercise what seemed to be an infinite capacity for being annoying. He was a poor advertisement even for the celebrity business. And what was celebrity anyway but what others bestowed? And that was it. You could be famous simply because people believed it, no matter how feckless, useless and downright bloody stupid you were. I looked across at my new son, sleeping peacefully and innocently in his mother's arms, and made up my mind. I was going to teach him that there was nothing special about being special, because most so-called special people were anything but. I was going to raise him to be an ordinary kid who would grow to be an ordinary man – a man with a decent set of ethics and a moral centre, one whose achievements and personality and conduct would speak for him. That's what he would be, nothing more and certainly nothing less.

Nobody special.

Laurel Beach

That night as the tide came in I thought I heard a voice from far out at sea, a thin, breathless, twisted sound borne on the pulse of surf like the faint snatches of music that sometimes break through the static between radio stations. That was all there was: me, darkness, the waves and that blurred, broken whisper. The door was closed, the curtains drawn, the lights out, my eyes screwed tightly shut. I was alone, isolated and unreachable in my bland hotel room. The television was off, the phone unplugged, no mobile devices. There were no distractions. I'd been there many times but this was my first night in Laurel Beach. This time around, it was the first night. I was there to remember the last time, to try to make sense of it. But not quite yet. This was the deep breath before the dive.

I listened and wondered what the voice, little more than the decaying echo of human speech, was saying. It might have been a desperate but pointless plea for help from someone drifting helplessly out into the dark depths, a prayer to someone's treacherous god, a confession, an angry accusation – perhaps a weather forecast or a news bulletin or even a poem. The words were fractured and indecipherable, perhaps uttered in a foreign language – too indistinct and distorted for me to tell if it came from the lips of a man or a woman. All I could distinguish was cadence, regular as a heartbeat. It was even and calm, and it went on for a long time. It definitely came from beyond the window, from somewhere very far away.

After a while, I rose and opened the curtains, gazing out at the street below, lit with yellow-orange lights and dotted with toy people going to or staggering from the late bars. Along the way hotel signs poured sickly neon stains across the scene. Then I looked at the wide beach and the sea beyond. More lights rose and fell with the tidal swell, yachts and pleasure cruisers at anchor out there, in the dark, above the depths. I hated it all, the leering lights and the laughing drunks, the swaying masts and cheerless hotels. I hated everyone and everything in this stinking town. I wanted it to split away from the land and slip into the bay, to slide down the continental slope, sink to the bottom of the Atlantic. I wanted to see those lights wink out one by one, and watch the drinkers drown, and drown with them. This town had killed me once and I wanted payback.

The surge of hatred left me as abruptly as it had arrived. It wasn't Laurel Beach that was to blame, was it? The town was merely where it had happened, where the unthinkable had taken place. The motorist doesn't hold the tarmac responsible for the tailgating idiot who rams him from behind. The fighter pilot doesn't curse the sky for the missile that takes him down. Yet the town was by no means wholly innocent of my metaphorical demise. Locations come to reflect the nature of their inhabitants. This was a place of transients, losers and gamblers, and a magnet for those who profited from their follies and vices, their infinite need. It had played its part.

The voice had stopped by then. I kept on listening, though. The hotel was utterly silent. Then I realised that I couldn't even hear the incoming waves. There was no reason I should have. The windows were triple-glazed against the chill winds that blew in off the sea in winter, and the heavy drapes completed the soundproofing. All I could really hear was my heart, banging slowly like a funeral drum; a high-pitched, rhythmic whistle that was probably the blood coursing through my veins; and a deeper note that was only the ebb and flow of breath. It's the true soundtrack of life. Most people only notice it when it stops.

I also realised I was cold, as chilled as a corpse on a slab. That gave me a different kind of shiver so I walked to the bathroom and took a piss, more to prove to myself that I was awake than to empty my bladder. I didn't bother checking myself in the mirror. I already knew what I looked like. No reminder was necessary.

Back in the main room I opened a bottle of water and rummaged in the suitcase for a pack of paracetemol. I popped two tablets, just in case I was going down with something, not that I cared a damn about sickness or health. I was prepared for anything, but whatever happened I didn't want it to go down with me feeling like shit. I smoked a cigarette then crawled back into bed and closed my eyes, losing myself in aimless thought that always seemed to return to the same event, that which had driven me away all those years ago, and which had brought me back at last, back to the last place in the world I ever wanted to see again. Eventually, the memories and regrets and morphing faces blurred into a slapstick cartoon with a Carl Stalling soundtrack and, when that hypnagogic entertainment wound down, at last I fell off a cliff and into the abyss of dreamless sleep.

The next day I overslept and awoke to heat and blazing sunshine. The dining room was closed so I went out for a long, leisurely walk along the promenade, hoping to find somewhere that sold decent coffee and maybe a cooked breakfast at a reasonable price. I was hoping for something else, too – something that could never be found, no matter where or how hard I looked. The past is not so much a foreign country as a continent sunk beneath the waves, its bricks and mortar and trees and bones scattered by irresistible currents, lost forever. Remembering is like marine archaeology, and just as dangerous, the drowned ruins infested with razor edges, unseen predators and toxic surprises. One false move can mean disaster. It simply isn't safe. But I looked anyway. What else was I to do? After all, it was why I was there.

The beach was already dotted with a wide variety of body shapes and an equally diverse range of beachwear. There was plenty of female flesh on display, most of it spread on towels and blankets, white and pink and brown bodies, cooking in the sun. Milk, lobster and caramel; dishes of every shape and size. Small groups of hungry-looking young and not-so-young men threaded their way through the smörgåsbord. Some of the women, the oldest ones or those with male and sometimes obvious female partners, were passed by. Single women or all-girl groups were looked over, carefully assessed, occasionally spoken to. I looked too, but I didn't see what I wanted. I would never see that again.

I guessed the strollers were just window-shopping, though they would surely not have been averse to sampling the wares on display if they received the least encouragement. But they were out of luck. It was too early in the day. Maybe later, after lunch and a glass or two of wine. Definitely much later, when the sun worshippers grew tired of soaking up UV and sunblock, and hit the seafront bars in earnest. Then, many would get what they wanted – an hour or two of strings-free fun with a tanned, toned, sun-bleached chancer. Some would get a little more than that – planted seeds or an embarrassing infection, perhaps an incurable, life-changing one. The combination of sun and alcohol makes people stupid. Stupid people make bad decisions. That's a lesson I learned the hard way; though it would be more accurate to say that someone else saved me the trouble. One evening of too many cocktails; one wrong, flippant word; one moment of uncharacteristic petulance; one short, angry walk into eternity. The shark was already there, waiting for the opening that would eventually come. I saw him talk to her as she left, only a couple of words that elicited only what at first seemed to be silence, though the message must have been written all over her face and confirmed in her eyes. She looked back at me once, not with affection, pushed the door open and vanished into the gaudy, noisy night. He quickly finished his drink and followed. I don't know what happened next. I never saw her again. No one ever told me.

I stayed there for a week, observing the hunters and the

hunted on the beach, always alert but never called into action. Relief and disappointment were one and the same. I didn't know what I would have said or done if I found what I was looking for. Would I even recognise those faces after such a long time? Every time I look in the mirror I am reminded of how the years change our features, complexion, posture and demeanour. I'm not the same as I was back then, not by a long chalk. But was I ever who I think I was? The currents in that lost continent are deceptive and the sands shift constantly, obscuring landmarks and obliterating footprints. By the time we get round to recalling ourselves, the face in mirror belongs to a stranger. A drowned man who still needs to breathe.

So each day and night I walked the promenade from one end to the other, sitting at tables outside empty cafés, drifting into overbright bars and darkened nightclubs. I ignored the raucous stag parties and the smaller, quieter groups of workmates and friends out for just a drink or two to unwind after a stressful day at work. I sidestepped the gaggles of stumbling, ridiculously costumed women on hen nights, the youths clustered outside amusement arcades, the office and factory girls and boys out on the pull, the tired families and wired beanos from further inland. I politely deflected unsubtle approaches from women not quite sober enough to notice that I wasn't much of a catch but not yet too far gone to hold a clumsily flirtatious conversation. I tuned out the ritual catcalls and lewd suggestions exchanged by gangs of revellers, the shouts and squeals and screams that always erupt when men and women and alcohol collide in quantity, turned away from the brawls and inebriated threats, the shuffling dancers, the puking and the falling.

Only a watcher – a hunter in my own way, I suppose – I wasn't part of this desperate, uneven race for oblivion and the kind of fun that would only be remembered on smartphone screens, maybe drunkenly shared on Facebook or Instagram, perhaps vaguely and regretfully recalled in a discreet clinic a week or two later. Joining in the game was wholly unnecessary. Besides, I'd already lost all self-respect just by coming back to Laurel Beach.

Every night, in that lonely space between getting into bed and sleeping, I heard the waves and the spectral voice they carried. Sometimes it came more than once, but never more than four times in the course of any one night. I strained to hear but could make out nothing. It became no clearer, no louder. The message remained elusive. It shouldn't have been audible – it *couldn't* have been – but it was undeniably there. I didn't care what it was trying to tell me, if anything; I didn't want to know the source. For all I knew it was a mermaid, a ghost, extraterrestrials, a drunk sprawled singing tonelessly in a dinghy, an aural hallucination like the disjointed voices and sudden explosive noises you hear sometimes just as you're nodding off. Perhaps it was God speaking to me in the language of Heaven. I didn't give a fuck who or what it was. I just wanted it to stop.

And so the week went by in a blur of faces, bars and sand, and the nights of coloured lights and bad music merged into a single, prolonged assault on my senses. One evening – I forget which – at dusk, in a blessedly quiet fish restaurant, dawdling over poorly cooked chips and a tasteless pie that bore little resemblance to the advertised cheese and vegetable, I thought I saw someone familiar sitting at a corner table with a man who looked a bit like I might have done once upon a time. But when I stood, about to go over and make a fool of myself, I saw they were total strangers, and that man was as different from me as it was possible to get. It was only when I left that I realised I'd been to the restaurant before, that time I first came to Laurel Beach, and the pair occupied the same table at which we'd once dined. The food had been better then. Everything had been better. It had been the night before the last night, before the empty wardrobe and vanished suitcase – before the irrational guilt of the betrayed fell upon me like an immovable cloak.

After the restaurant I moved away from the seafront, melting into the maze of narrow, barely-lit streets woven between the town's main roads. As I wandered through those lanes and alleys, one more shadow among so many, it felt as though I might at any moment catch a glimpse of my younger self a little way ahead or to one side, or perhaps hear my own laughter, the rise and fall and brief pauses of the kind of conversation long denied me. But I saw only people I did not recognise, heard only voices that were not mine. All I saw of myself on those walks was the darkness of obstructed light, and my tongue was mute.

Everyone in this place, I realised as I returned to the hotel, was a spectre. All the things they did there were to prove to themselves that they were alive. The lemming solar cult, the manic drinking and the desultory fighting, the photographs and souvenirs, the empty holiday stranger-fucks – it was a ritual designed solely to affirm continued existence. And they were mistaken. If they really needed it so badly, they were already dead.

Like me. Like us. Like then.

On the seventh morning, after one last night of phantom voices and disturbed sleep, I packed my suitcase and checked out of the hotel. It had been a futile experiment. Memories are not reality, and no act of remembrance can bring the past to life. Yesterday can never be recaptured. We may look at its remains and recall names, faces, sensations and events – but photographs and memorabilia are mere fossils, impressions of what was. They are not the thing itself, only empty containers like the scavenged shells piled up on an unforgiving shore, dead things like the ammonites and trilobites on display at the local museum – like a man roaming alone through a seaside town in the height of summer, searching for what he can no longer have.

It was a grey, muggy, overcast day. Out at sea there was no visible horizon. I wondered if it might rain, but I was leaving and didn't care one way or the other. As the train pulled out of the station I thought I saw her on the platform, looking just as she had, dressed the same way. She was alone, of course. Whoever she was, she was alone. Then the sun came out from behind the clouds and she wasn't there at all. Another shadow cast from memory, vanishing with the light. And, I realised with shocking clarity, she was another thing I no longer cared about.

I leaned back in my seat and closed my eyes, daydreaming, fantasising once again that the town slipped into the sea, imagining the sudden stillness after the waves finally swallowed the top of the tallest building. It was no more than the place deserved. It was, after all, an embodiment of my past, a failed memory that could no longer be replayed with exactitude. Constantly remembering and reliving the past eventually destroys the memories, the way tape recordings become worn and stretched and brittle with time and use, until all that remains is the idea. Maybe that's what ghosts are, the spaces left when everything else has been eroded to nothing.

A thought struck me. Was that what the indecipherable voice had been trying to tell me? That all I am now is a void marking the place I once occupied? It made a kind of sense, but at that moment, as the train gathered speed and ate up the track and Laurel Beach was left behind, sunk now beneath the ocean of time, I didn't give a damn. The ghosts might linger on – but the haunting was done. The town and I were finished with each other. I was never going back.

The Minder

I've been having problems with the calendar lately. Dates fall on the wrong days, months don't follow the standard order. Some weeks are longer than others, some far too short. Even the year seems to vary according to the weather, my mood or what's on television. Old memories are fresh in the mind; the later ones are hazy and obscure. Now and then they swap places. It's my age, I suppose. Only to be expected. Mental decay advances at a different rate to physical deterioration but at some point they're bound to converge, if you live long enough. This is my time, when the brain begins to throw in the towel and the other organs rapidly follow joints and muscles on their depressing journey down the toilet of senescence. When I look in the mirror I see a ghost, grey of skin and what remains of my hair, someone I barely recognise and often wish I didn't. Soon enough there will be no one to see, no one to look. I think it might be a relief.

    I should tell someone, now, while I still can. I've thought of doing so many times in the past weeks but either could never find the right person or was unable to put the words in an order that made any kind of sense. Now, I'm not sure it really matters who I tell or how I do it. No one will believe it anyway. I know sometimes even I don't. But it has to be told.

I'd known Atkinson from school. We were in the same form, the same house, played together in the rugby and cricket teams. We weren't exactly friends but maintained a cordial relationship based on mutual respect, shared enemies and the team spirit drummed into us from the moment we first entered the school gates. Like all the other boys, we pretended to despise the grammar school ethos while secretly soaking it up. The school uniform meant more than any of us would ever admit. It gave us an identity, a common purpose. You didn't have to like a fellow pupil to accept him as a peer and a person of the right sort, even when he wasn't. But Atkinson was, by general consensus, a good, solid chap – unspectacular but dogged, bright but not brilliant, as loyal as they come. He did well at school, went up to Oxford and did well there, a First in history. Like most successful officers, he was a resourceful man but not an imaginative one. At school his best subjects had been the sciences, maths, technical drawing, woodwork. He liked structure, method and established procedure, rules and regulations. He thrived in the school hierarchy, in teams. It was no surprise to me that he excelled as a soldier. He was made for military protocol, to give orders and to obey them. Oxford was followed by Sandhurst. From there Atkinson went on to serve in Aden during the last year of the British administration, Northern Ireland, Cyprus, the Falklands. He acquitted himself well in the Falklands, by all accounts – a couple of minor medals, a mention or two in despatches, a promotion to colonel, whispers of elevation to brigadier.

Then, without warning, he seemed to vanish. Unusually, there were no rumours. In 1983, at the annual school reunion, Atkinson was conspicuously absent. We talked about him, of course, but only to try to make sense of that abrupt end to what seemed destined to be a long and glittering army career. Yet we had nothing to work with. There was no suggestion of any kind of impropriety, no hint of scandal or wrongdoing, no known health, relationship or financial problems. Indeed, it was clear that he'd led an exemplary life, as a soldier and as a man. One chap a few years younger than me, a lieutenant in Atkinson's regiment, thought there might have been some sort of accident during an exercise on Salisbury Plain shortly before he disappeared from view, but to his certain knowledge there had been no damage to either equipment or personnel, and it was unclear as to whether Atkinson had been involved at all. Another chap suggested Atkinson might be involved in something hush-hush, undercover work somewhere. But he had no evidence to offer in support of that. It was a mystery.

That's how it stayed for another year, until one bright summer Saturday evening in 1984 when I made the mistake of stepping into a pub in Epsom for a pint of beer to quench a thirst honed to perfection by a morning of weeding, mowing, pruning and digging, followed by a few repair jobs, then a couple of afternoon hours wandering through supermarket aisles with the wife. With the garden tidied, the shopping stowed away and – best of all from my point of view, as I was a little worn down by the unaccustomed exertion – my better half off to visit the mother-in-law, I yielded to temptation and strolled round to my local boozer. There was a good chance one or two of my old cronies would be there, playing darts or putting the world to rights over a foaming glass or two. I took the *Times* and a pen along, just in case, which was just as well, as my luck was out in more ways than one. The place was empty apart from two taciturn youths mechanically feeding coins into a one-armed bandit, and a man and woman in their late twenties or early thirties engaged in the sort of animated but whispered conversation that suggested an illicit liaison.

Disappointed that my friends had apparently found something more important to do on such a fine evening, but determined to imbibe at least two pints of London Pride as recompense for working on my normally sacrosanct Saturday, I took my first beer into the pub's garden, selected one of the empty tables, and sat down to have a go at the cryptic crossword. As usual, it seemed beyond my intellectual capacity. The first clue was all the clue I needed to tell me I was probably wasting my time: *Kent smuggler on half time? Line one takes him to London. There's a coincidence! (13)*. I struggled with that for a while, finished my beer and bought another. Just as I was about to give up on the cruciverbalism and move on to actually reading the newspaper, a shadow fell onto the page and someone spoke.

'Howard? Is that you? Will Howard?'

I looked up, squinting because the sun was now high and right behind the speaker's head, so I was unable to make out the face. The voice sounded vaguely familiar but I couldn't quite place it. 'Yes, I'm William Howard. I'm sorry – do I know you?'

I still didn't recognise him at all when he sat opposite me. The stooped, scrawny man looked even older than I am now, more than thirty years later. The suit was four decades too young and two sizes too big for him. His hair was long but lank and thinning, brown thickly streaked with grey; his scarred face was lined and wrinkled bags hung below his eyes, the whites of which were yellowed and bloodshot. His liver-spotted hands trembled as he placed his drink – a large whisky with what to my discerning gaze appeared to be the merest splash of soda – next to mine. I was a bit alarmed that this battered old boy seemed to know me, though he was at least clean and presentable.

'It's me,' he said, his words slightly slurred. 'John Atkinson. We were at school together. Remember?'

'Atkinson? Good Lord,' I responded, not believing for a second that it was really him. In 1984 I was only forty-three years old. This fellow must have left school years before I'd even been born. There was no way he could have been my old classmate. I couldn't have hidden my disbelief very well. He picked up on it immediately.

'Yes, I know I look different, older. I've had a – a difficult time. I'm not well, you see. Not well at all.'

I gazed at him more closely. The lines of his face seemed right, as far as I could remember. The voice was more or less the same as the one I'd last heard twenty-three years earlier, if you ignored the throaty rasp and the slur, which probably owed as much to cigarettes and whisky as to age or illness. Yet I still couldn't bring myself to accept this wreck of a man as my old friend. But then he grinned, and it was the one I recalled so clearly – the expression Atkinson wore when we played rugby or cricket, the one I'd seen so many times it had become indelibly printed on my memory.

I was horrified. 'Jesus Christ, Atkinson – you look bloody dreadful. What on earth happened? Do you need help? If there's anything I can do, you only have to say the word. Money, a good doctor, you name it.' There it was in all its glory – the old school tie, something that is more than a strip of cloth and which binds all who wear it in ways most of them could never define. It's not called a tie for nothing.

Atkinson stared at me for a long, uncomfortable moment, a fraction longer than would normally be considered polite. 'I think I'm past any assistance a banker or physician could offer,' he said quietly. Then he grinned again. 'Or a psychiatrist, for that matter. What they said at the inquiry – well, it doesn't matter. I'm sane enough, I think. Not well, that's undeniable. But not mad. They knew that. Because they couldn't explain it either.'

I was bewildered. 'I'm sorry, Atkinson – I'm not following you.'

'No, you wouldn't,' he said sadly. He looked down at the table, opened his mouth as if to say more, shook his head. Then he looked me in the eye, as if trying to read my thoughts. Finally, he seemed to come to a decision. 'There is one thing you could do for me, Howard.'

'What's that?'

'Listen,' he said. 'Please, just listen.'

'Do you still watch science fiction films, Howard? I remember at school you were always going to the pictures to see films like *Forbidden Planet* and *This Island Earth*. Well, has it ever struck you that the science fiction vision of tomorrow is always only yesterday with added whistles and bells? Look at that film *Blade Runner* – back to the ancient Middle East, pyramids and ziggurats. *Metropolis* was an Art Deco nightmare. *A Clockwork Orange* was filmed on a modern housing estate that was already dated. Either the styles and fashions of the day, already fading into history, or the architecture of long ago are augmented with pipes and cables, silver paint, neon tubes and plastic laminate, escaping steam and scavenged rubbish. The writers are as bad. When Wells looked into the far future he saw brutal troglodytes and a gentle but decadent Classical-style culture – primitive cannibals and effete Graeco-Romans. Further still, he saw life receding back into the sea, the last word in nostalgia.

'We look backwards to find what we will become. Take any post-apocalyptic vision and you'll find refuge in a return to pre-industrial tribalism, an older kind of social order. The future is always a cliché, a distorted copy of what is or has already been. And on those rare occasions when the visionaries see something other than post-catastrophic return to prehistory or a dystopian version of yesterday, they see us at the mercy of beings with god-like powers, to help or destroy us as they see fit. When we think of the future we retreat to the familiar comfort of religion, though now God has become an astronaut or a mutant – or we wallow in repressive, authoritarian regimes that remind us of our schooldays. Science fiction is never really about tomorrow.

'Why is that, do you think? Well, I'll tell you why. It's because the alternative – the truth of what might be – is too awful to contemplate. I found out the hard way.

'It began late one evening in the April of 1983. I was in charge of a detachment of recruits on a routine training exercise – night combat. The objective was simple. My team had to take control of a command post set up in a wooded area not far from Salisbury. And we had to take it by stealth. I was the CO but I left it to the lads to determine strategy and improvise, only offering occasional advice. They were a good bunch and they did well. We worked our way around field boundaries without being spotted, detoured and double back on ourselves to throw the "enemy" off the scent, crawled on our bellies across open ground, then entered the woods, spread out to minimise casualties, moving from tree to tree. There was a bit of a mist among the trees – you remember how it used to be after dark at the old school, that copse at the far end of the playing fields, where they abutted the farm? It was just like that.

'The further we walked into the woods, the more spaced apart we became, the less noise we made. The command post was somewhere in there and other team would be waiting for us, that was certain. After a while I realised that either the woods were much deeper than I'd thought, or I was somehow walking round in circles. The trees just seemed to go on forever. I couldn't hear a damned thing – not a whisper, not the sound of a snapping twig or a boot through fallen leaves, nothing. Either my boys were rewriting the book on stealthy movement, or they'd stopped moving at all. I didn't have any choice but to keep going. The temperature had dropped, the mist was thicker, and I was lost. I saw no reason to panic, though. Sooner or later I was bound to either bump into someone or come out of the woods.

'Eventually, I saw a light ahead of me. I thought it must be the command post. By then I was bloody sick and tired of the whole business. I was cold, tired and hungry. I decided to go toward the light and try to take the damned post on my own. At least if I was captured or "killed" someone would give me a cup of tea and maybe a good, hot meal. Then I was out of the trees and the light was – daylight. And I was in a real war zone.

'At first I thought I was hallucinating, or maybe I'd fallen asleep and was dreaming. There were men running around, Arabs or Turks by the look of them, yelling in a language I didn't recognise. Bullets were tearing into the buildings around me, slaughtering men where they stood. It was obvious they were amateurs. They didn't have a clue. Just stood around frozen, waiting to die. I stood there for a few seconds, then my training kicked in. I yelled at the men and waved them into buildings, behind walls, anywhere. I found myself holed up in a burned-out bar with five lads, no more than twenty at the oldest. One of them spoke English. He understood what I was saying and started translating my instructions for the other men to hear. They didn't ask who I was or question my authority – all they wanted was someone to take charge, to tell them what to do. I didn't question the situation either. I simply did what my training dictated, regardless of who these boys were or who was shooting at them. I picked up a dead man's AK47 with an almost-full magazine, and took command.

'I still don't know how we fought our way out of there. All I really remember is that somehow we found ourselves in their base, among friends. I sat down with their leaders, was given coffee and bread, and discovered, through careful questioning and a few white lies, that I was in a place called Tikrit, somewhere in Iraq. The boys I'd joined were Kurds, some outfit called peshmerga, who were fighting the Daesh, an enemy they described in the sort of terms we would use for the Nazis. They weren't too surprised to encounter an English soldier – and certainly nowhere near as surprised as I was to actually be there – as there were a number of British and other European volunteers fighting alongside them.

'Then I had my second surprise, the biggest one of all. The peshmerga were visited by a French television crew. I kept out of sight until they left, and got hold of a newspaper one of them had been reading. It was *Le Figaro* and the front page news was about a plane crash in the Alps, a German passenger jet that had been deliberately flown into a mountain by its co-pilot. And according to that same front page, it was the year 2015. I was stunned. I could accept that somehow I'd made my way from Wiltshire to Iraq, maybe after a bang on the head and amnesia; but surely the journey hadn't taken nearly thirty-two years? There was an old car, riddled with bullets and all its tyres shot to ribbons, but with one miraculously intact wing mirror. I was, I admit, almost afraid to look. But when I did pluck up the courage to inspect my face in the mirror, I was astonished to see that I hadn't aged a day. I hadn't just travelled all that way in the blink of an eye – somehow, I'd also travelled through time, into the future.

'I didn't know what to do at first. I kept hoping that I'd wake up in my own bed and find it had all been a dream – or maybe I'd come to lying on a woodland floor with a large bump on my head from where I'd walked into a tree in the dark. Every time I slept or closed my eyes for even an instant, I prayed that when I opened them again I would see a good old English woodland scene. But it wasn't to be, Howard. Every night I went to sleep in Iraq and every morning I woke up there. It gradually dawned on me that I was technically a deserter, and that I had an impossible story to tell. I'd either be gaoled or thrown in an asylum. It was clear that I couldn't go home under my real name. I took the only course that seemed open to me. I stayed with the peshmerga, ate and fought with them, and was accepted by them as a fellow warrior in their fight with the hated Daesh.

'And a bitter fight it was, too. My time in Ulster was nasty in many ways, Aden could be pretty hairy, and I saw some terrible things in the Falklands. But the Daesh were – will be – the worst enemy I have ever faced. They were ruthless, fanatical, callous and sadistic to a fault. They called themselves Muslims but many of the peshmerga were also Muslims, and they loathed the Daesh. They had good reason. I saw Kurdish and Arab boys and girls – children, Howard – who had been raped, tortured and disfigured. The Daesh butchered whole villages, enslaved women to sell or use for sex, forced people to convert to their appalling perversion of Islam or die, destroyed ancient art and monuments. When I saw and understood what the Daesh were doing, I resolved to stay on and fight them. I stayed with the peshmerga, in Iraq and Syria, fighting what at first seemed a successful campaign but which soon turned out to be a ragged retreat. No matter how many we captured or killed, more seemed to be flocking to join them.

One day, in the course of one of our occasional pushes back into Daesh territory, we temporarily liberated a small village. I say "liberated" – but there's only so much liberation corpses need. The Daesh had slaughtered all the men, beheading or burning them alive, and herded all the women and girls into a house where they – no, it was too awful for words. I won't describe it. When we entered there was only one Daesh fighter left to guard the few survivors, a boy of no more than nineteen years old. He spoke English, said he was from Yorkshire, Bradford. He seemed proud of what he and the other evil bastards had done. I shot him in the head, Howard; executed him on the spot. I hope you won't think badly of me for that. But if you'd seen what I saw – well, I suppose God will be my judge, though I'm no longer so sure of the Almighty's existence.

'What I'd seen, what I'd done – it sickened me. I had to get out while I still retained some sense of morality. A few months after I arrived, a comrade introduced me to a couple of other Brits, who knew some Americans, who knew a Dutchman with connections. He arranged a fake Dutch passport for me, my peshmerga friends gave me some US dollars. I crossed the border from Iraq to Turkey, travelled from there to Bulgaria and back to the UK. I wangled a job in the personal security business, became a minder for celebrities who today are still in nappies, and a few who aren't yet even twinkles in their fathers' eyes. I learned about the world of 2015. In some ways it was a wonderful age, with marvellous technology and medical miracles. But a dreadful darkness was rising, Howard. Environmental catastrophe was looming, total economic collapse seemed to be unavoidable, and religious fanaticism was a constant source of trouble. Western politicians were either corrupt and self-serving or unbelievably stupid, and corporate greed was rampant. The Daesh had equivalents and allies in Africa and across the Middle East and elsewhere. It was a war conducted both by organised armies and small groups of terrorists, and it was escalating.

'While I was in London things got worse. Within two years there were biological, chemical and conventional bombings in almost every major city in Europe and the United States, in Australia and India. A major war was raging across Africa, the Middle East was in flames. The Arab states of North Africa fell to them, one by one. Only a fragile, unlikely alliance between Turkey, Israel, Iran and India stood between the Daesh and the whole of western Asia. That alliance had support from the West, and from the Caucasian states, but despite the regular terrorist attacks only those countries on the front line had any stomach for open confrontation. I think the fools in Washington, Westminster and Brussels thought they could negotiate with the Daesh. Well, there was no chance of that. It was chaos. The world was living in fear – and the bad guys were winning.

'I went back, of course. The peshmerga were fighting on, despite losing most of Kurdistan. I felt a degree of affection for them. They had been my first comrades in my new time, after all. They had welcomed me, accepted me as one of their own. I owed them. In April 2017 I was leading a mixed detachment of Kurds, British and Irish volunteers, and former members of the Iraqi regular army. We raided Daesh strongholds in Syria and Iraq – now part of the Daesh so-called Caliphate. In August that year I stopped a bullet with my shoulder just outside Damascus and was forced to recuperate in Tehran. The Turks, Russians and Americans escalated their involvement but were too busy squabbling among themselves and with the Syrian regime, still clinging on by its fingertips, to do any more than worsen the chaos.

By the middle of 2018 the North African branch of the Caliphate – what was once Libya, Tunisia and Egypt – was launching attacks by air and sea along the European Mediterranean coast and into Israel. In Pakistan, only Karachi and Islamabad remained under government control. Afghanistan was taken over by the Caliphate's allies, the Taliban. Bangladesh, Malaysia and Indonesia were in the grip of civil war. There was unrest among Daesh supporters all over Europe, fighting on the streets between radicalised Muslims and nationalist factions, terrorist bombings, random acts of murderous brutality. Then some bright spark in Pakistan realised he had control of a nuclear missile installation, told the latest Daesh Caliph, a German fanatic who'd been treated for paranoid schizophrenia in Berlin before seeing the light and changing his religion. I was in the Kurdish mountains, taking a well-earned breather with my unit, when the mad bastard pressed the button.

'They went for their traditional enemies, naturally. Tel Aviv and New Delhi, Haifa and Bombay were vapourised. Israel and India didn't bother resetting for new targets before responding. It was goodbye to Karachi, Islamabad, Baghdad, Damascus, Tehran, Cairo, Riyadh and Mecca. Iran replied with the nukes it claimed not to have. The Yanks, always good for a knee-jerk reaction, panicked when they saw the mushroom clouds. They too targeted their traditional enemies, the Russians – the Soviet Union begins to disintegrate about ten years from now, by the way – North Korea, and China. The Russians and Chinese retaliated by bombing Europe, Australia and North America. North Korea, also using weapons it wasn't supposed to have, attacked South Korea and Japan. The Third World War lasted less than three days.

'After that, things got worse, a return to barbarism, like that old science fiction film you used to rave about, *Things to Come*. But there was no advanced civilisation in Iraq to come to humanity's rescue – only the Daesh reigned there. They took advantage of the chaos, the long winter that followed the war. What was left of Europe became a battleground. I took my peshmerga lads and volunteers there. We fought in the ruins of Athens, Rome, Florence, Geneva, Marseille…

'And we failed. We retreated and watched as they vandalised and raped and killed. We looked on, helpless, as the Italians and Greeks either accepted conversion or were put to the sword. Then we moved further north, fighting every inch of the way. We had no news, no supply lines, no support. We scavenged weapons and ammunition, clothing and food. There were rumours, heard from half-crazy refugees and the occasional hysterical radio broadcast – the Russians, demoralised and decimated, had surrendered. The United States had splintered into a thousand different factions squabbling over the smoking ruins of its cities and the radioactive prairies. The South American nations had closed their borders, fearing disease and sedition. It did them no good at all. Old diseases swept the continents, new ones appeared. Crops failed across the world. Trade was abandoned in favour of piracy and self-sufficiency. In what was left of Britain, the Daesh sympathisers and anyone who might be one had been brutally eliminated, but the country was controlled by feuding warlords and gangsters. I've no idea how much of what we heard was true but it was clear that millions were dying of radiation poisoning; millions more were starving or freezing to death – perhaps billions. And we continued to kill one another, just to survive in a world that was no longer fit to live in. It went on and on, for years, then decades. The rumours dried up as the population dwindled. The airwaves fell silent.

'About a year ago, by my timescale, I was still leading the remnant of my peshmerga unit. There were only half a dozen of them left, two Kurds, a Scottish chap and three Germans we'd picked up along the way, I forget where. We were staying in a small village in the Pyrenees, a farming community that had hired us to protect them. It was like *The Magnificent Seven*, except that we were all old men and could barely lift a rifle between us, let alone fight. But we were all the village could afford. We worked for a roof over our heads, bad bread, and goat stew. By then we considered that the lap of luxury. The few travellers who came by, tolerated if they moved on quickly and weren't threatening, but treated with suspicion and never welcomed as guests, told us the Daesh were no longer a threat – every homicidal lunatic in Africa and what was left of the Middle East was proclaiming himself the true Caliph and they were too busy issuing fatwas against and beheading allegedly apostate rivals to bother with their old ambitions. Besides, there were few of them left and hardly anyone still alive to conquer. No, all we had to worry about were neighbouring villages, which occasionally launched raids on each other for livestock and women. They were inexperienced at warfare and had only the odd shotgun and a few old pistols, while we had our AK47s and a few boxes of grenades. After the first few attempts, they gave us a wide berth.

'Inevitably, as the long winter continued and supplies dwindled so we too embarked on a life of banditry. We began attacking our neighbours, taking what they had so we could live. It was a bad business but we didn't really have much choice. One night, we were launching a sneak attack on a village a little further away than usual – by then the nearest ones had nothing left for us to steal and in any case were all but abandoned – when we entered a bank of fog in a narrow pass. We went cautiously, fearful of ambush and anxious about the unfamiliar terrain. Suddenly, I found myself alone in the dark, unable to see a damned thing. My comrades didn't answer when I called. Then I was through the fog and staring at a group of lads from my old regiment, standing there in a field in Wiltshire. Somehow I'd returned to the very same spot I'd left from, only an hour or two after I'd departed for the future. It was 1983 again.

'There was a bit of consternation about the way I'd suddenly appeared out of nowhere, in the midst of a group of squaddies. But in true army fashion they ignored the facts of my arrival and took me in for questioning as a possible terrorist or spy. I was savvy enough to play along so I just gave them the usual – name, rank and serial number. Well, that really threw them. Although I no longer looked much like the photographs, my fingerprints and blood group matched those on record. The result was a hasty – and highly unofficial – enquiry that endorsed my claim to be who I said I was, agreed that it would not be in the country's best interests to put me up before a court martial for desertion, and arranged for me to be have my army pension. The alternative, I suppose, was to do things by the book and risk raising a lot of awkward and disturbing questions. That's the way the army does things, Howard – like all organisations with a lot of history and a craving for public adulation, it is adept at sweeping things under carpets, burying them deep in remote holes, or just pretending everything is normal. The official record shows that I was given an honourable discharge due to illness.

'What did I tell them? I told them nothing. The head-shrinkers they brought in tried to catch me out but I stuck to my guns. As far as they are concerned the last thing I recalled before I reappeared was walking into the trees during that exercise, the night I disappeared.

'After that, they cut me loose. I had savings and the contents of a current account to add to the pension. I also had the family house – that three-storey place in Esher. Well, obviously I couldn't live there without the neighbours wondering what the hell was going on, so I sold up and bought myself a little bungalow. I'm a bit old for stairs now, Howard – even though I'm technically still the same age as you.'

That last remark was said with a small, boyish grin that left his sad old eyes untouched. Wordlessly, I rose, went to the bar and bought another pint, with a single malt for Atkinson. I remembered that he had always been fond of a sly nip on the coach home from rugby matches against other schools. We sat in silence for a few minutes, then he spoke again. 'Well, what do you think?'

What could I say? I didn't believe a word of it. Whatever freak disease was ravaging his body and had turned him into an elderly man years before his time, it had clearly affected his mind. But I pitied him. Whatever else might be said of me, I've never been one to kick a man when he's down. 'It's an interesting story,' I said eventually, opting for diplomacy, though scepticism must have been written all over my face.

To my surprise, he laughed. 'You don't believe me. And I can't blame you. It's a fantastic tale, after all. If anyone had come to me with such a story only two years ago – in your timescale – I would have told him to bugger off and get a grip. Well, all I can do is tell you what happened, the way it happened. At least you listened. That was good of you, Howard. I'm glad I found you here at last.'

With that, he drained his glass, sighed appreciatively, and stood, stiffly and in evident pain. 'Oh yes,' he said with a grimace, stretching and rubbing his lower back. 'I've been keeping an eye out for you. I knew you lived round this way, but I couldn't remember the address. I guessed if I visited the local pubs regularly I was bound to run into you sometime. You see, you *will* believe me one day, Howard.'

The sun was almost gone. In the half-light he looked tired, frail and weighed down, like an old builder's labourer who'd carried one heavy load too many. He raised a hand in a weary kind of salute and was gone before I had the chance to say another word.

That was thirty-one years ago. I never saw him again. A couple of months later I received a telephone call from another old schoolmate who'd seen a death notice in his local newspaper. That was a month or so after the event. The funeral had been and gone. Not that I would have attended – I have always tried to avoid funerals. Death was going to find me sooner or later and I've never really fancied rushing to confront it. I was sorry to hear he'd died, of course. But I was also rather relieved. There would be no more awkward encounters with poor Atkinson, no more forced smiles and insincere nods as I listened to the ravings of a man at the end of his rope, not for me or anyone else. As far as I was concerned, his death was a kindness. He'd been spared the indignity of wider scorn and had escaped the subtle ostracisation that so often accompanies mental illness in people of our social class.

After that, I simply got on with my life. I grew older, made more money, divorced and remarried, was well thought of at the bank, the Rotary Club and the parish council. When my second wife died, I decided to retire. God knows I hadn't needed to work for several years, but I liked the social life that went with it, and I quite enjoyed my job. With my children grown up, married off and scattered across the country, I was alone and free to do what I liked. So I focused on my golf handicap and my local community responsibilities, and made the most of whatever spare time I had by broadening my cultural horizons. I spent a lot of time in London – art exhibitions, museums, plays, concerts, even touring the city's old churches. I thought of Atkinson every once in a while, but less often as the years rolled by. At some point I stopped thinking about him at all. Even his crazy, doom-laden descriptions of supposed future events receded to the very back of my mind and stayed there, undisturbed. Until one Saturday last month.

That morning I'd been taking a look round St Clement Danes in the Strand, followed by a lunch coffee and cake in a nearby branch of Costa, when I made a snap decision to take a stroll up to Marylebone to visit the Wallace Collection, which was on what I nowadays feel obliged to call my 'bucket list'. On the way I would pop into Foyle's, perhaps have a quick pint somewhere now that the late September sun was firmly and undeniably over the yard-arm. That day I was feeling my age. After Foyle's I stopped to take a breather in Soho Square, just a few minutes on a bench to give my aching knees and back a rest. While I was sitting there, a young woman walked by, yapping into a mobile phone. For a moment, I thought she must be a prostitute who was doing well for herself – far too much make-up, a skirt that left very little to the imagination, enough gold on her fingers, round her neck and hanging from her ears to make Fort Knox do a stock-take, the kind of walk that used to be a hallmark of the oldest profession. She wasn't on her own, though. A few discreet steps behind her were two tough-looking men in black suits, their eyes everywhere but on her – unlike mine, I must confess. Then I recognised her from the newspapers and television, the kind of minor celebrity who's done nothing much to shout about but is portrayed as a superstar. I supposed the two suited men were her bodyguards, what they call minders. The woman stopped and said something to one of the men, who fumbled in his jacket pockets and produced a packet of cigarettes and a lighter. While he lit a cigarette for her, the other man continued to scan the square. Then he met my gaze and held it.

We both started – me because Atkinson was still only in his early forties; him because he saw the young man I had once been beneath the time-worn body I now inhabited. For a moment, I couldn't breathe and Soho Square seemed to contract and spin around me. I wanted to scream myself sick but somehow managed to pull myself together. Atkinson was frowning, his mouth open as if he was about to speak. Then he shook his head, smiled in that tight, slightly embarrassed way people have when they've mistaken a stranger for someone they know, and curtly nodded in my direction before returning his attention to possible threats to the actress or pop singer or whatever she was. I sat paralysed and speechless as the trio went on their way across the square to wherever they were going. All thoughts of the Wallace Collection driven from my mind, I stumbled into the nearest pub and drank enough beer and whisky to stupefy me for the train journey home. Unfortunately, when I awoke the next morning, I remembered everything.

And that's why I'm getting this off my chest now. Because in that moment I remembered everything he'd told me in that pub garden so long ago, all the things I'd forgotten about his story. Seeing him in Soho brought it all back to me, as clearly as if it was only yesterday. Everything fell into place. If he was telling me the truth that day – and now, thanks to the daily news and that unexpected meeting, I have every reason to accept that he wasn't a mere raving lunatic – then we have maybe a year until all hell breaks loose and humanity flushes itself down the toilet. I'm not worried for myself. From what the doctor tells me I'll probably be dead by then. But it will be a shame for the innocents who will suffer and die when the time comes, especially the children. After all, none of it will be their fault.

Atkinson was right in another way. There are no crumbs of comfort in what is to come – no return to Eden or the womb, no parental figure to rescue us from our steep decline and put us back on the path to progress, no deity to save us, no interstellar intervention. All we have before us are cruelty, disaster and rapid decay.

I yearn for an old-fashioned future, like the ones we used to have.

Nature in the Raw

Numbers were up with the heatwave, which everyone agreed was a very good thing. So too, unfortunately, were disputes. Tempers grew hotter, keeping pace with the rising mercury and falling lager levels in the clubhouse kegs, and there had been one actual stand-up shouting match – between two ladies, for heaven's sake. It was, as their mild-mannered yet formidable president said almost hourly, bloody intolerable. Robinson wasn't quite sure if he was referring to the heat or the increasing fractiousness but supposed it didn't really matter in the long run. The two were as inextricably linked as conjoined twins. The real problem, as far as Robinson could see, was the sudden influx of new members. Now the club boasted nearly eighty newcomers and social relationships were constantly shifting, divisions becoming more sharply defined. The increased income from subscriptions did have one unforeseen and unarguable benefit, though – the bar was now very well stocked.

He sucked iced Pimm's through a plastic straw. Just the ticket on a day like this, though it was somewhat lacking in alcohol content for his taste. He could see the president now, talking to one of the new recruits, a middle-aged woman who would, Robinson thought a little uncharitably, have been better advised to join a gym. She was not exactly a sight for sore eyes. And she was a Barefooter, which from his point of view was a bit unfortunate, though it could have been worse. He sighed, yearning for the old days when he knew everyone and numbers were too small for schisms.

Membership had long been stagnant but in recent years there had been a steep decline as people grew old and died. From nearly forty in the late 1980s, by 2012 there were only six members left. There had been talk of winding up, selling the property and giving the proceeds to charity. Unsurprisingly, they had all agreed to that, if only because the question of who actually owned the patch of woodland was rather murky. Initially, it had been a joint purchase by the founding members, with an agreement that ownership belonged to the club. Therefore the land, with its trees, pond, trails, picnic areas and clubhouse, was the property of whoever was a current member at any given moment. It was written into the club's constitution, or so they all thought. But consultation with a solicitor led to the revelation that the constitution didn't matter a damn when set against English law.

Now the president was chatting to one of the Pogonophiles. Robinson was intrigued. He helped himself to another jug of Pimm's and observed them closely. The Pogonophile was gesturing, waving an arm in a circle as if to encompass the club's land. This did not look good.

Solicitors had advised that the land and all its contents were actually the property of the signatories or their heirs. That meant selling it off would mean lengthy and complex negotiations with the sons and daughters of deceased members, and it could be expected that some at least would want a slice of the pie. The remaining members had discussed it over a few drinks and unanimously decided to quietly drop the idea and hope the problem would somehow just go away. With the expanding membership it was bound to rear its ugly head again. Robinson, always suspicious of any sort of change, wondered if the burgeoning membership was really down to the heat, or if word was getting around that joining the club was potentially a shortcut to a windfall.

However, 'signatories' was a loaded word. One solicitor argued that it encompassed all members, their signatures on membership application forms being sufficient to entitle them to a share. The constitution did not define 'signatories'. Further legal advice indicated that where a word was not defined in a contract or other document, its ordinary dictionary definition would apply. Yet there was also the question of intent – what did those who drew up and agreed the constitution mean when they included that word? Robinson couldn't remember and nor could the others. Plenty of water had passed under the bridge since then, not to mention countless brandies, whiskies, gins and vodkas, and more than a few beers. The issue would need to be argued in a court of law and decided by a judge. That would cost money. It might go to appeal, which would cost a lot more money. Appeals to higher authorities might ensue, in which case everyone could wave goodbye to getting their hands on a decent share of the property's value, as it would all be swallowed up by legal costs.

Out of the clubhouse window Robinson could see the president now had a cluster of members around him. And some non-members, as Robinson liked to joke after a few drinks. One of those was a newcomer, a rather attractive woman in her late thirties, a brunette whose adipose tissue was arranged in a spectacular and exciting fashion. She was causing quite a stir among the members. These things happened sometimes. It was only natural. At that moment Robinson himself was not unaffected. Fortunately she was a Fundamentalist, as those with what he saw as traditional views were now calling themselves. She was a happy-go-lucky sort – liked a drink, too, which to Robinson's mind was always a good thing in a woman. Standing next to her was another woman, a scrawny blonde the wrong side of fifty, who he identified as a Bottomer. Robinson shook his head and made an incoherent grumbling noise. Why were Bottomers tolerated at all? On that matter the rules were crystal clear. The woman and all her ilk – there were only three of them, all women, but that was beside the point – should be disbarred and not allowed back until they conformed to that basic requirement.

The debate among the president and those surrounding him was growing heated. The Pogonophile was posturing aggressively, chest puffed out and fists clenched, leaning so his face was only inches from the president's. The Bottomer placed a hand placatingly on the Pogonophile's shoulder but it was shrugged off and he turned to her, unclenching one hand and poking a finger rudely toward her face, an unmistakeably masculine way of emphasising a point. Robinson shook his head again. The man was like a stag in the rutting season. Everything he did spoke of territoriality, testosterone and sexual dominance. That was a laugh. The president outranked him in the membership hierarchy in more ways than one. And obviously the Pogonophile didn't know the president was a karate black belt.

Now everyone in the group was shouting and waving there arms around. Except for the president, of course – the man had never been known to lose his temper. Robinson considered going out there to try to calm things down a bit, but decided to have another glass of Pimm's instead. Furtively, even though there was on-one else in the clubhouse to see him, he added a large shot of vodka to the drink. Nobody would have cared but he didn't want the other members to think he was a drunk. Like all drunks he didn't quite understand it was a bit late for that.

It had started with the Barefooters, Robinson foggily recalled. That had been fine. The rule on footwear was both sensible and flexible. *Footwear of any kind may be worn to protect members from harm or discomfort.* Who could take issue with that? Yet some newcomers had, claiming it violated a key principle of what they called the Movement. Old or new, most members had been baffled by that. They were unaware of any Movement and were sure they didn't actually belong to one. Alarmingly, the Barefooters had been joined by the Bareheaders, who took issue with hats, again in defiance of the rules. *Headgear may be worn to protect members from the effects of strong sunlight or to prevent unnecessary loss of body heat during unusually cold weather.* It was there in black and white, and was, once again, sensible and clearly intended to benefit members' health. Who could argue with that? But argue they did.

After that the arguments and divisions increased and escalated. The thankfully all-male Pogonophiles claimed it was essential that a Movement – that word again – aimed at replicating the original, innocent and untainted condition of humanity should forego shaving. Early Man, they reasoned, was hirsute and that was the way Man was intended to be. Ergo, members should leave their chins unscraped and their hair untrimmed. Robinson particularly disliked these macho types, who always seemed to be reading Hemingway and someone called Robert Bly. One of the men had tried to convert him to his version of the Movement, earnestly telling him about a life-changing story called *Iron John*. When Robinson sarcastically remarked he'd read the story as a child and thought it was a fine fairy story, the strutting apostle of facial hair had been doubly offended. Fortunately there were few of them, though they did have tacit support from a couple of female members whose armpits made the Forest of Dean look like a desert.

Tempers outside had finally frayed to breaking point. The Pogonophile shoved the president hard in the chest, not sufficiently hard to be called violent but a clear act of aggression. The president gave him the first of three warnings – not strictly canonical in Oriental martial arts, Robinson knew, but the president was a kindly man who liked to give assailants the chance to back off while they could still walk unaided. The Bottomer placed herself between the two men, presumably believing a feminine intercession would calm things down. In that she was sadly mistaken. The Pogonophile thrust her aside and she fell, yelping in pain as she landed on her knee. That too wasn't quite an act of violence but it was close enough. The president issued his second warning. A Barefooter woman, another blonde, who had come along to see what all the noise was about, said something to the Bottomer, who glared and gave her the finger. Words were spoken, offence taken. Suddenly the two women were rolling around on the ground, scratching, screeching and pulling hair. Robinson hadn't seen who struck the first blow, and it had happened so suddenly that it was unlikely anyone else had, which might be tricky if a disciplinary hearing called for an eyewitness. The Pogonophile said something to the Barefooter, some sort of encouragement. The president issued his third and final warning. Calm and serene, his Zen-like presence had been one reason he had been elected president. He was just the sort of person who could be relied upon to maintain harmony and peace, and bring a conclusion to any dispute. It helped that people were slightly afraid of him.

The Barefooter was now sitting on the Bottomer's chest, like someone riding a horse while sitting the wrong way. It reminded Robinson of a couple of videos he'd downloaded from the internet. Just as it had been in those, the Barefooter woman tugged the garment from the Bottomer's lower body. That's where the similarity to Robinson's leisure viewing ended, though. She threw the bikini bottom at the Pogonophile, who ripped the offending item, not quite in half but enough to make it unwearable. The Bottomer shrieked in outrage. The Barefooter laughed, but the sound turned to a scream when the other woman bit her buttocks. The Pogonophile turned to the president and tossed him the ruined item, following that with an obscene gesture.

Robinson was troubled. Although he loathed the holier-and-hairier-than-thou Pogonophiles, he had to admit it was only right that the Bottomer should be compelled to abide by the club's central rule, the one that encapsulated what they were all about. *With the exception of footwear and headgear, and prescription spectacles or protective sunglasses, no clothing whatsoever shall be worn at any time. Where a medical or physiological condition requires that a member must temporarily wear a garment, they shall not attend the clubhouse or the surrounding grounds until that necessity is past. For the purposes of this rule prosthetic limbs are not clothing.* Still, that was no way for members to behave – and certainly not ladies.

To his horror, Robinson saw two Edenists approaching the turmoil, a man and a woman. The two male Edenists were a sort of extreme branch of the Pogonophiles, and had formed couples with women whose under-arm and pubic hair was so profuse it could probably be styled like topiary. These four flagrantly and regularly flouted another of the rules. *Members shall not engage in sexual activity or any form of intimate physical contact while on club premises. Married or otherwise established couples may hold hands but kissing is forbidden. Greeting other members with a handshake is permissible but greeting with a hug or a kiss of any kind is not.* These people believed wholly in a return to the animal-like innocence of Early Man, like that of the Garden of Eden, and had sex anywhere and often, though in the face of protests and complaints they had lately confined their conjugations to the deeper recesses of the shrubbery. Now the male Edenist was siding with the Pogonophile against the president, and more finger-thrusting and fist-waving was taking place. This was going to be good. Robinson added more vodka to his

Pimm's and sat back to enjoy the fun.

Encouraged by reinforcements, the Pogonophile was becoming even more aggressive. Then he crossed the line separating hale limbs from plaster casts. With a sneer even his untidy beard could not disguise, he slapped the president's face – not hard, but a blow nonetheless. The Edenist stepped forward to add threat. That was two bad mistakes in the space of a second. What followed was a cartoon-like blur of hands and feet lashing at vulnerable body parts. In less than a minute the Pogonophile and the Edenist were lying on the ground, groaning and seemingly unable to decide whether to tend to their sore limbs, their bruised faces or their aching testicles. The Edenist woman was screaming hysterically, no doubt wondering if the fracas had jeopardised her chances of an afternoon quickie in the bushes. The president calmly bent to help the denuded Bottomer to her feet, gallantly offering his beanie hat so the woman could cover her pubic region. He really was an old softie.

This unseemly incident, Robinson realised, would have repercussions. He foresaw a meeting, discussion about tightening and clarifying rules, and – best of all – a couple of expulsions. The rule on fighting was unambiguous. *Any member who initiates violence against another member on club premises, for any reason, shall be expelled permanently. Their membership rights shall cease immediately and their annual subscription shall be refunded on a* pro-rata *basis. The use of reasonable force in self-defence is permissible.* That would reduce the number of offensive members to the tune of one Pogonophile and one Edenist, probably two of the latter, as the Edenist's partner would surely resign her membership when her man was unceremoniously kicked out; and the other Pogonophiles and Edenists, no doubt friends of the downed men, might even do likewise in protest. Excellent news all round. The Pogonophiles, as befitted their nature, were the newcomers most interested in the question of who owned the land. Getting rid of them would bring a little peace. He certainly wouldn't miss their continual pissing at strategic points on the club's perimeter.

As Robinson was adding yet more vodka to his Pimm's and considering whether he should add a iced water and splash of lime cordial as a concession to both the heat and his own self-image as a non-drunk, the curvaceous Fundamentalist brunette entered the clubhouse. He sat down again and ran his eyes over her naked body, too drunk to care that she might notice his appreciative gaze. She gave him a sly smile and a wink as she too helped herself to a Pimm's and boosted it with an impressive dribble of gin. Despite the amount he'd had to drink Robinson once again felt that stirring. He'd always prided himself on being one of the club's more upstanding members, and that was now the literal truth. The woman sat next to him and flirtatiously touched her glass against his. Robinson self-consciously ran his hand over his chin, wishing he'd bothered shaving that morning.

On the other hand, maybe he should grow a beard.

My Torture Porn Hell

The photograph wasn't exactly flattering. She'd been snapped struggling out of a ridiculously long car with black-tinted windows, a too-short black skirt hiked up almost to her waist. The black shoelace masquerading as underwear left nothing to the imagination except the name of her waxing salon. With that awful *TOWIE* make-up job and absurdly low-cut top she looked twenty years older, quite a bit blonder and a hell of a lot cheaper than I knew she was. Her lips were frozen in a drunken grimace somewhere between a leer and a snarl. The pony-tailed guy in the creased tuxedo copping a feel of her left breast as he was supposedly helping her out of the stretch limo had wide, overbright eyes and a tight grin that had their origins somewhere in Colombia.

The front page was bad enough. But the feature on pages four to six was disastrous. It was illustrated with a barely-pixellated shot of my ex-wife, naked, gagged and tied spread-eagled to a bed, her face twisted in what looked like pain but might equally have been passion, a blur-faced, bare-chested man with tattoos crouching over her. And the headline – Christ, the headline…

MY TORTURE PORN HELL. Those four words said one thing to Joe Public but to Nathan Turpin they meant something else entirely, another four-word message: *MY CAREER IS RUINED*. Panic-stricken, I grabbed my phone. This required major-league damage limitation.

'Benedict? Have you seen the papers this morning?'

'Hi, Nathan. If you mean Bernadette's little stunt, yes. It was my idea, actually. Once she told me about the film I felt it was my duty to expose you and put a stop to your sordid games.'

I was bewildered. 'Film? What film?'

'The torture porn video, Nathan. The one in which Bernadette is serially abused by an assortment of drugged-up freaks. Look, we've always been friends and I admire you as an artist, but really. We've been through a lot and always stuck together. But I had no idea you were into that sort of thing.'

'Me neither,' I squawked. 'Benedict, you know damned well that me and Bernadette separated amicably. I treated her really well when we were together. She never had to work – I gave her whatever she wanted. When we divorced we split everything fifty-fifty, even though nearly all the money and property were mine. Christ, two days ago she rang me and asked if I wanted dinner at Langan's. I had a drink with her and Chrissie in the Groucho the week before last, for God's sake. Believe me, there was no torture film and the things she told the paper are all lies.'

'If there was no film, where did the video clip come from? Bernadette said it was one of the less revolting ones. But she described the rest in graphic detail. I nearly threw up when she told me about the big tattooed guy in the mask using that thing on her.'

'What thing?'

'You know what I'm talking about.'

'No, I bloody well don't. What thing?'

'I can't even bring myself to describe it.'

There was a pause in the conversation while I struggled to imagine what Benedict was talking about and Benedict maintained the sort of silence that was written in bold upper case.

'Benedict, is this some kind of sick joke?'

'You tell me, Nathan. I'll ask you again. If you didn't make a film of your ex-wife being tortured and abused by a bunch of perverts, then where did the stills from the video footage come from? No way was it faked. It's definitely Bernadette.'

'Yes, it's Bernadette. But those pictures didn't come from any film I made. We did make one home movie that I suppose you'd describe as X-rated but there was no torture and nobody else was involved. The film was made one night about three years ago when Bernadette and I had had a few drinks and she suggested playing a little game, thought it might be fun to get up to something a bit kinky. Yes, I tied her wrists and ankles to the bed with her stockings and I admit I filmed some of what we did on a digital camcorder. But it was all her idea, we were alone throughout and I certainly didn't use whatever that thing is that you were talking about. She definitely wasn't gagged. I don't even have any sodding tattoos. Bloody hell, Benedict – you've known me for years. I can't believe you think I'd do something like that.'

Benedict was silent. I prayed that my old friend – and

occasional personal publicist – would believe me. But the silence dragged on and my nerves began to fray.

'OK,' Benedict eventually spoke. 'Let's say I believe you. Let's say it was all as you said, and that as far as you're concerned you and Bernadette are still on good terms. Why would she come to me with a false story, one that's clearly designed to ruin your reputation? Why would she encourage me to negotiate a deal with one of the tabloids? It can't be for the money. The divorce was only made absolute a couple of months ago so if she got half your money from the divorce settlement then she must still be fairly comfortable. She's pretty famous in her own right, so it can't just be to get her name in the papers. So what's her motive for setting you up?'

Now it was my turn to remain silent while mental gears meshed and attempted to come up with an explanation. But the machinery came up short. I was stumped. 'Buggered if I know,' I said. 'But hang on a minute. Why did she go to you? She knows we're mates. I know you seem to have taken her side in this, but why go to you?'

'Well, to be honest I wasn't her first choice. Bernadette wanted Max to handle it, but – well, you know all about that. Anyway, he may be the best – OK, past tense – but I'm not that far behind. And technically you're not a client, Nathan. Whatever I've done for you in the past was because you're my friend, not a paying customer.'

'So Bernadette's paying you to do the dirty on me? Shit, what a cow. I can't believe it.'

'Sorry, Nathan. Business is business and I have bills to pay. Look, I didn't want to do it to you but, as I said, she had me convinced she was telling the truth. Maybe if you let me see the film you say you shot we could figure out some sort of plan that would save your reputation without compromising my professional relationship with Bernadette?'

I was scandalised. 'You must be joking. There's no way I'm showing you a video of me and Bernadette having sex. I'm very old-fashioned about that sort of thing. Anyway, I deleted my only copy of the file when we separated – thought it was the gentlemanly thing to do. I suppose she could have copied it before she moved out, but it certainly wasn't where that picture came from.'

'Or,' Benedict suggested, 'the film *you* reckon the clip was taken from never existed and she's telling the truth? I'm only saying what others might say, Nathan. You're a professional film-maker, man. And you're a hoarder. I know for a fact that you've still got all the stuff you shot when you were a kid, and some of it's so old it's on Betamax tapes. I wouldn't be surprised if you even had some nitrate stock in your cellar. Are you really telling me you didn't keep a copy for your personal archive?'

Benedict was right in one respect. Where my creations are concerned, I *am* a hoarder. I have back-ups and multiple copies of everything I ever committed to film, tape or digital video. I even scanned the old flicker-books I made when I was a kid, the stick-figures and cartoons that began my obsession with film. But I didn't keep a copy of that video. I really did delete it, and I never backed it up. That night we decided our relationship was a thing of the past, when Bernadette told me she'd moved on, I moved on in a parallel direction. That DVT film, the only record of our domestic eroticism, was deleted. I even burned the bloody tape on the barbecue in our back garden.

'Ben, has Bernadette ever complained about me before? I mean, about money, the settlement, the way I treated her, anything?'

'No, of course not. This is the first time she's ever made any accusations about you.'

'Did she say why she showed you the pictures?'

'Only that she wanted the world to know what a bastard you really are. I can't say as I blame her. It must have been dreadful living with a pervert like you.'

Oh God, he believed her. My old mate Benedict believed her story. We'd know each other since were kids, for Christ's sake. 'But you know I'm not a pervert, Ben. Remember your stag night? I wouldn't even go to that strip joint with you. And Harry's fortieth birthday, when I refused to come with you guys to the lap-dancing club? There's no gratuitous nudity in my films, no sexual skeletons in my closet. How can you believe her?'

There was another lengthy silence. Then, in a voice so quiet I had to strain to hear it, he said 'Because I remember Diana Etherington.'

Now it was my turn to be silent as I racked my brain trying to place the name. 'Sorry,' I said when the search of my internal database drew a blank. 'Is that name supposed to mean something to me?'

'Diana Etherington. The girl who lived next door to me in Willingdale Avenue. Blonde, not very pretty. Pigtails? Had the brother with the stammer?'

The mists cleared. 'What, little Didi? God, I'd forgotten all about her. What do you mean, not very pretty?

I thought she was OK, apart from the ears. But what about her?'

'I caught you playing doctors and nurses with her. She had her pants off and you were looking between her legs.'

'Bloody hell, Ben – I was five years old. It's what little kids do, healthy curiosity. Anyway, I know for a fact that you did the same with my sister the year before, and she was a year younger than us.'

'You were nearly six, Nathan,' said the hypocritical bastard, his voice oozing counterfeit innocence. 'That's a big difference. And your sister put me up to it because she wanted me to show her mine. Anyway, all I'm saying is that you have a track record.'

'So what are you going to do about it? Tell Operation Yewtree that Didi Etherington next door took her knickers off for me when I was six? They'll tell you to fuck off. And do you know what? That's exactly what you *can* do.'

Hanging up on Benedict didn't make me feel any better. Calling Bernadette made me feel worse, much worse.

'Nathan? I thought I told you to stop phoning me?'

'Eh? You rang me a couple of weeks ago to give me your new mobile number. In fact, you've called me several times since then. Remember the drinks with Chrissie? Bernie, what on earth is going on?'

'If you've read the papers you know what's going on. I'm exposing you, you bastard.'

'But I haven't done anything,' I protested. 'I thought everything was OK between us. Why did you say those pictures came from a film I made? And why have you been telling all those lies about me?'

She actually growled, a screech like a cat defending itself against something bigger and nastier. 'Lies? I've only told the truth. That film was disgusting. I couldn't believe it when you tied me up then brought all those blokes in. I'll never forgive you for that, Nathan Turpin. That's why I copied it before I walked out. Now the whole world knows what a vile, perverted scumbag you really are. Now fuck off and leave me alone. One more call and I'll take out an injunction.'

I would have been speechless even if I hadn't had only the dialling tone to converse with. Was this the woman I'd spent twelve more or less happy years with, the person who'd actually tried to talk me into giving her *less* money in the divorce settlement? It made no sense. Only two weeks before, we'd been getting drunk together and remembering old times. There had been a brief moment when she looked at me the way she had when we first got together, a look that made me wish things could have turned out differently. Chrissie had remarked on how well we were getting on and even called us 'the lovebirds', which for once did not seem intended as sarcasm.

Mind you, it's always a bit tricky trying to work out what Chrissie means when she says something. I've known her for nearly ten years and I still can't work out if she's a lipstick lesbian, a well-turned transsexual or a highly convincing drag queen. At various times she's claimed to be all three, and once confided that she was an ordinary, straight woman putting on an act. That was at a party where according to rumour she ended up in bed with the hostess, but only after she'd drunkenly tried to get me into the sack; and only a couple of days before she loudly announced that she was flying to Los Angeles for the final phase of her sex change, though I know for a fact that she really went to a cottage in the Lake District to finish one of the pornographic novels she writes under a *nom de plume* that for all I know could be her real name.

'Nathan, darling,' she twittered when I called her. 'You are a dark horse. I must say I feel left out. I would have *loved* to be in that video. I have this bijou rubber and leather outfit with a built-in dildo. It's bloody *huge*, sweetie – wouldn't be out of place on a shire horse. I'm sure Bernie would have found that *très amusant*.'

She sounded too loud, too shrill. I was immediately suspicious, and a bit disappointed. 'Chrissie, have you been at the coke again? You told me you'd given up. That was why we paid for you to go into the Priory, to get cleaned up.'

Chrissie was affronted. 'Coke? Darling, how *dare* you? I have *not* been using coke again. Honestly, not one tiny white flake has passed my nostrils since I came out of rehab.'

'Sorry,' I replied. 'It's just that you sound a bit, well, *hyper*.'

'Oh, *that*. No dear, it isn't coke. I've been trying out this new stuff called crystal meth. Makes you high as a kite and as horny as a bitch in heat. Fancy coming over for a bit of you-know-what? I could wear that little number I was just talking about.'

It was obvious that sensible – or even decent – conversation was the last thing I was going to get from Chrissie. But with the mood she was in I wouldn't have been at all surprised if she tried to give me something else. I made a mental note to put the security chain on the front door before I retired for the night and, in time-honoured fashion, made my excuses and put the phone down. No sooner had I done that than the bloody thing rang. With a despairing sigh, I picked up the receiver and identified myself.

'Mr Turpin? Nathan? Richard Pruitt, *Daily Mail*. I wondered if you might like to give your side of the story, now that your ex-wife has gone public about your bedroom romps.'

'Look, Mr Pruitt – Richard – all I have to say is that I did *not* make the film my ex-wife says I made, OK?'

'Fair enough. Then where did those stills come from?'

'I have no idea. They're not from the film I did make.'

'I thought you said you didn't make the film?'

'I *did* make a film – just not the one Bernadette says I made.'

'So the stills she reckons are from the film you made...'

'...are from another film entirely, that is correct.'

'So why don't you release the real film and let everyone judge for themselves?'

'Because even if I was willing to let the public see a movie of my ex-wife and I having sex – which I'm not – I couldn't anyway because the film no longer exists.'

There was a pause as Pruitt strove to construct a response. Suddenly, I knew exactly where this was going.

'So if your film no longer exists, and you didn't make the film the pictures are from...'

'...then where did Bernadette's pictures come from? All I can say is that they're nothing to do with me. And in any case, the film I did make was destroyed.'

'Why would you need to destroy the film if it was as innocent as you claim?'

'Because it showed Bernadette and I having sex,' I pointed out, aiming for a reasonable tone though barely able to remain even remotely calm. 'I thought that it would not be appropriate to keep it once our marriage had ended. The film was of Bernie and myself, no one else. There was no torture, no violence, merely a bit of light-hearted role-play.'

'What about that bloody great big –'

'It never happened.'

'The bloke with the tattoos?'

'It was just the two of us. No other bloke, no tattoos.'

'The butter?'

'Butter?' I hadn't read anything about that.

'Butter, like Marlon Brando used on what's-her-name in *Last Tango in Paris*. You know, I've always thought "Last Tango" should be rhyming slang for one up the – '

'No dairy produce whatsoever,' I hastily interjected. 'It was just me, Bernadette, a bed, a pair of silk stockings, a bottle of wine and a digital video camera. A married couple having a bit of consensual fun in the privacy of their own home, at night, with doors locked, the curtains closed, and no other participants or onlookers. No foodstuffs, gags, artificial aids or stimulants; no special outfits, prosthetics or other bodily modifications.'

'Christ,' said Pruitt disbelievingly. 'You're a right boring bastard, aren't you? No wonder she gave you the elbow.'

I didn't get much sleep that night. But I did get the glimmer of an idea. When I rose from my miserable duvet early in the morning I logged onto Amazon and downloaded a few titles to my Kindle. I didn't bother checking the news. The prospect of more of the same from Bernadette was just too bloody depressing. I didn't go into the office either, despite needing to make important calls to the moneybags who had promised funding for my next film and whose feet were probably candidates for permafrost after the previous day's headlines.

Chrissie's books were short, little more than novelettes, but surprisingly well-crafted. I'd expected chaotic and kaleidoscopic non-stop sex scenes from the author known to her – OK, or *his* – fans as Messaline Duprée, but what I got were characters, beautiful writing and interesting plots. Yes, there was still plenty of sex – the sort of long, graphic descriptions of unbridled and eye-popping carnality I would have expected from Chrissie – but they were both literate and readable. I read the first two before lunch.

I found what I was looking for halfway through the third book. *Servitude* was a strange tale about a bored housewife's extra-marital flings with an assortment of unlikely strangers which, I realised with a start, was actually a retelling of a medieval romance, Chrétien de Troyes' *Perceval*, the story of the quest for the Holy Grail. In Chrissie's version, the heroine Persephone is a downtrodden, pretty but dowdy woman, kept that way by her wealthy, domineering husband, who convinces her that she really is the simpleton he keeps telling her she is, that a woman's place is in the home, and so on. One day she opens the door to a ginger-haired man standing for the local council as an Independent Socialist, to whom she responds by regurgitating her husband's Tory views. The man argues with her, she invites him in, and they indulge in a spot of dialectic, Persephone ultimately allowing him temporary ownership of the means of production. I recognised that scene immediately – it was the one early on in Perceval where the hero has a tussle with a mystery knight in red armour and sees him off by shoving a spear into his eye, a Freudian moment Chrissie of all people was bound to spot. Of course, in Chrissie's version the scene was tweaked to suit her own purpose. As a film-maker I would probably have done the same.

Persephone's encounter with the Red Knight gives her a taste for adventure and soon she actively goes out of her way to engage in infidelities with – for her – a range of exotic types. But the bit that grabbed my attention was an extended sequence beginning when Persephone opens an envelope mistakenly delivered to her house. The letter inside is to advise the addressee that she has been successful in her audition for a part in a forthcoming film. It gives a date, a time and a location. Persephone, by now up for just about anything, decides to go along in the aspiring actress' place. When she arrives, she sees that the place is a rather grand mansion. The people there don't seem to notice that she isn't who she's supposed to be. They give her a costume to change into – merely a set of skimpy lingerie – and apply some make-up. Then she's shown into a large room containing cameras, lights, two other women, an array of sex toys, and a large bed. The porn shoot is a parody of Chrétien's description of the ritual procession in the Grail

Castle. It culminates with Persephone bound and gagged on the bed while a sado-masochistic orgy unfolds around and on top of her. Finally, instead of the Grail in Chrétien's story, which is borne in by a young woman and has a lance held over it and dripping blood into it – Sigmund would have approved – there is a ceremonious entrance by a muscular, masked and tattooed man, who is not only physically well-endowed but is also brandishing an enormous – well, I think you get the picture. Needless to say, the tattooed man's implements give Persephone the biggest orgasm she's had in her life; and while she's transfigured in ecstasy the lights go out and the scene ends. Which is pretty much how it is for Perceval in the original.

The story resumes with Persephone hungry for more of the same. But when she makes an uninvited return trip to the mansion, she finds a very posh elderly couple who have no idea that their home has been used to shoot porn movies while they were sunning themselves in the Algarve. Bitterly disappointed, Persephone undertakes increasingly risky sexual escapades in an attempt to somehow recreate that day of agonising bliss. However, unlike Chrétien's story, which was never completed, Persephone stumbles more or less by accident into a shoot by the same film company, starring the same muscular stud. This time she takes the lead, puts on a real show, and demands and gets a regular job. She tells her husband she's leaving him and walks out of his life and into a career as a porn star.

I finished the book pretty well persuaded that all medieval knightly quest stories were in fact gender-bending allegories of women's search for sexual fulfilment. And I was wholly convinced that this was where Bernadette had got her inspiration. I rang Chrissie – there was no way I was risking Bernie's wrath again – but only connected with voicemail. Benedict, according to the estuarine young lady who answered his phone, was in conference with a client. Frustrated, I steeled myself to look at the previous day's newspapers again. Just who was that creep manhandling Bernadette as she practically fell from that car? He looked vaguely familiar. Who was that bloke with the tattoos?

And then I had it. I found a magnifying glass in my desk drawer. The man groping Bernie out of the limousine had a curl of tattoo just visible through his open-necked shirt – a snake of some sort. The masked man in the film stills printed in the newspapers had what seemed to be an identical design toward the top of his chest. Same build, same haircut – same man. I was right.

I began to put two and two together. Hadn't Bernadette always said she'd love to be in films? I was well known but I'd long been aware how much she longed to be famous in her own right. Despite the generous divorce settlement I thought the money might not last her very long. She had expensive tastes. As for Chrissie, she was always going on about how her books would make great movies. I knew she was dropping large hints to her good friend who also happened to be a bona fide film-maker, namely myself. But I'd never been keen on the sexploitation genre so had always cleverly – or so I thought – steered relevant conversations toward safer waters.

Then there was Benedict. Our friendship may have had its roots in our earliest childhood but I didn't need to be told that he was a venal, unscrupulous viper who'd pimp his own mother out for a decent payday. He'd certainly sold me down the river on Bernadette's behalf.

That was the whole equation, of course. A drug-addled author desperate for a film adaptation; a resentful woman craving stardom; a devious, greedy publicist. Result – one publicity stunt with a semi-famous film director as fall guy. I almost rang my solicitor. But then I had a better idea.

Over the next few weeks the scandal continued almost unabated. Whenever it looked like dying down, Bernadette would offer the tabloids further revelations and more stills taken from my alleged film. I was the recipient of an injunction to stop my non-existent pestering of Bernadette – also leaked to the media – and a letter from Bernadette's legal team demanding surrender of the film I hadn't made. I was regularly doorstepped by reporters, and deluged with phone calls from my rapidly-dwindling financial backers, asking me what the hell was going on and did I really expect them to maintain their association with a man of my despicable character. I responded to all of this with silence and the occasional 'no comment' – which of course served only to make me look more guilty.

I did wonder why Bernadette, Chrissie and Benedict were doing it. After all, any man in my position would crucify them in the press and in the courts the moment their sleazy little film was released. Calling Bernadette was out of the question, but Chrissie and Benedict refused to either answer or return my calls. It wasn't a major stretch, though. They all knew me very well indeed, well enough to know that I'd be reluctant to slog it out with them through the tabloids – which I despised – or the courts, which I firmly believed should be employed to administer justice, not settle sordid disputes between people who should know better. Besides, the publicity value would be immense. The film would be a sensation and make them shitloads more money than I'd ever get out of them in damages for defamation.

As it happens, I had a mate who worked in the seamier side of the film industry, a cinematographer who'd developed a heroin habit and paid for his gear by shooting hardcore movies in a succession of seedy Soho studios, hotel rooms and rent-by-the-hour flats. Once a good mate but latterly both a professional and social liability, Frannie owed me a few favours, and quite a bit of cash. A couple of weeks into my ordeal he contacted me to confess that he'd been the cameraman. According to Frannie, the film was produced and directed by a London porn baron and former actor appropriately named Rod Lancelot, who just happened to be a muscular bloke with a lot of tattoos, including one on his chest that he was proud of, a snake with a distinctly phallic head. The film itself was still being edited and was scheduled for release on DVD in a month or so. It had, so Frannie said, been an unusually soft-porn affair for Rod Lancelot, with a lot of non-sexual scenes and dialogue written especially for the star, the former Mrs Turpin – soon to be Mrs Lancelot, apparently – who Frannie claimed couldn't act her way out of a paper bag. That was news to me – she'd apparently been putting in Olivier-worthy performances in our marital home for years.

Frannie was just the man I wanted to hear from. He had access to everything I needed to plan my revenge. The only thing to be settled was the price, and Frannie had already injected most of that.

First, I told a few gossipy friends that I was working on an experimental film and would be out of circulation for a while. Then, true to my word, I made my film. I used outtakes from what was essentially Frannie's private porn collection, all those little bits that are discarded and ultimately deleted. Nowadays major film and television studios keep them to compile 'blooper reels' as DVD extras. The porn industry forgets all about them. You'll never see the fluffers struggling to get the leading men up to scratch, the premature ejaculations, or the erased segments where one bloke takes over from another who's too knackered to carry on. You won't see the bits where an actress bites down just a little too hard, or long fingernails accidentally slice into a man's most delicate parts. You will be spared the scenes that are abandoned halfway through because the actors simply don't fancy each other enough to get it on, or everyone's tired and uninterested and it's just plain boring for all concerned. Frannie had hundreds of hours of the stuff. Well, they were exactly what I wanted, as many items as possible, an astonishingly varied selection.

I spent a fortnight examining and choosing, another month editing and splicing. I looked for hair colour, physical build, background. I selected women who could pass for Bernadette from the rear or from particular frontal angles, and who wore garments and lingerie like those I remembered from her wardrobe; and scenes with men whose faces and other distinguishing features couldn't be seen. I chose scenes with backgrounds that resembled rooms in my house. I inserted footage of Bernadette from the many non-erotic home movies I'd made. It's amazing how slightly slowing down footage of a woman laughing can make them look as though they're in mid-orgasm. Perhaps that's why so many women say they like men who make them laugh.

It took another week or so to make sure my fades and jump cuts worked, and that there was no way any of the actual porn actors could be identified. Everything was done by careful editing and insertion. Nothing was Photoshopped. By the time I finished I had an hour-long porn compilation featuring women who appeared to be Bernadette having explicit, unsimulated sex with a dozen different men, seemingly in our bedroom, the living room, the kitchen, and on the stairs. I made bloody sure none of them were Rod Lancelot. One guy was carefully chosen for a vague resemblance in profile to Benedict, whose face was added from my home movies. He was the one lustily servicing the stitched-together Bernadette doppelgänger on the kitchen table. Just as well that good old Benedict always liked to hang out close to the booze supply at parties – that took care of the background – and that he loved a good splash-around in our jacuzzi. Plenty of useful flesh to work with. I would have put Chrissie into the mix somewhere but I honestly didn't know which sex to fit to her face.

When I was satisfied that the film was indistinguishable from any professionally shot and edited porn movie – and, just as importantly, that even I would have been hard-pressed to swear it wasn't really her – I put together titles and credits: *My Torture Porn Hell*, starring Bernadette Turpin, with made-up pornstar names for the faceless male actors. Benedict was the only man to get a face-check, under the name Judas Smallwood. The directorial credit went to Alan Smithee.

As a kind of courtesy, I made one last attempt to talk to Benedict. I called him early on a Sunday morning, when anyone who knew me would expect me still to be in bed after a late night at the editing suite. Benedict knew me well, so he answered the phone expecting me to be someone else.

'Hi, Benedict,' I greeted him cheerily. 'It's me, Nathan.'

'Nathan,' he echoed warily. 'You're up and about early. To what do I owe the pleasure?'

'Actually, I just wanted to tell you I have no hard feelings over the Bernadette business. I mean, I know you have to earn a crust. And let's face it, if it hadn't been you it would have been someone else, maybe someone who wouldn't have gone so easy on me, eh?'

'Well, that was the least I could do in view of our long friendship,' he lied. 'I must say I'm glad you're taking it so well. Most other people in your position would be after my blood.'

'Not at all,' I assured him. 'It's one of the hazards of being in the public eye. You can't really control how people see you. Anyway, who was it who said there's no such thing as bad publicity?'

'I think it was me,' Benedict joked.

I laughed dutifully. 'Besides, we're both professionals, Ben. We should be able to separate work from friendship so that one doesn't affect the other. For instance, if you were an actor in one of my films I'd have to put our friendship aside to get the best possible performance from you. And in a professional relationship you accept that sometimes things just have to be laid on the table.'

'Quite so,' he agreed. 'That reminds me, Nathan –

rumour has it you're working on a new film. Is it true?'

'For once the rumour mill grinds accurately,' I replied. 'I put the finishing touches to it last night, as a matter of fact. It's an experiment, not the sort of thing I usually do. I think it turned out quite well. It's about a woman's search for happiness, told in a series of symbolic episodes. Your wife will love it.'

'Sounds exciting,' he said. 'Well, if you need a publicist, you know where to find me. When will it be shown?'

'Oh, very soon. Anyway, got to dash. I'm supposed to be finalising the distribution today.'

That afternoon I took a bus to Soho, where one of Frannie's dodgier acquaintances administered a free porn site, and slipped him a hundred quid to put my film on the internet straight away and mention Bernadette's name in connection with the film in a couple of tweets. Then I went home and waited for the phone to ring. It was a surprisingly short wait.

Flowers in the Rain

At the door he stopped and looked back. They were sitting there chatting calmly and contentedly, continuing their conversation and drinking their wine as if nothing had happened. None of them raised their eyes to track his departure. He realised that in the time it took to walk the three yards between the table and the door they had shuffled round to erase the gap he'd left. There were no gestures of farewell. No one saw him out. None said goodbye. His transition from lounge to street did not register. He'd already ceased to exist. This would be the last time.

So that's that, he thought, standing in the drizzle. The road surface seemed unnaturally bright with the reflection of street lamps, headlights and shop signs – that hypnotically blossoming, constantly shifting night-glow he'd always loved, especially at the tail-end of a good night out, with a few drinks inside him. The luminosity of happy times. Well, there would be no more of that.

Years of friendship down the drain, all because of one mistake that wasn't even my fault. It was a betrayal of the worst kind – a blanket refusal to acknowledge the presence of a man they knew well and to whom each owed a debt of some kind. A loan he'd never asked to be repaid; a spot of painting and decorating here and there; pitching in with removals; running one of them to the hospital; giving advice and help whenever he could and wherever it was needed. *I've never troubled them for anything in return. I didn't do those things to impress anyone. They were my friends and that's what you do for your friends, you help them out when they need it. You're always there when they need someone to just be there. They'd do the same for me, wouldn't they?*

No, they wouldn't.

Numb with misery, he walked to the nearby bus stop. Several bunches of withered, bedraggled flowers were tied to the post. Someone had smashed the plastic cover and torn out the timetable. The pavement was littered with cigarette butts, empty cartons and paper napkins, well-gnawed chicken bones scattered like a bad augury. No one was waiting so he guessed he'd just missed a bus. It was late and the regular service would have finished by now. There would be a night bus along eventually, but he didn't know when. He didn't know if it mattered any more. He would get where he was going, that much was certain.

Even Sonia, he thought, Sonia, whose tears he had dried countless times, who had enlisted his help to cover up her disastrous affair with a man at her office and had persuaded him to lie to her partner Doug, a false alibi so their relationship could be saved. She, his friend since they were both at primary school, had avoided his eyes and turned her face away when he tried to tell them what had really happened. Like the others, she hadn't looked at or said a word to him, not even as she opened the door to admit him to her home, where he discovered the dinner party he hadn't been invited to. Like the others, she had ignored him thereafter. What he said wouldn't be heard and it wouldn't be heeded. The jury had already deliberated and come to the obvious conclusions. Judgement had been passed and sentence pronounced. There would be no appeal.

I didn't know.

Ignorance is no defence.

It was a mistake, he told the fried chicken shop across the road, still open but empty and hungry for customers. It had once seemed irresistible, finger lickin' good. Chicken coated with breadcrumbs and herbs, a secret recipe.

For him, a recipe for disaster.

He leaned against the bus shelter, head spinning and temple throbbing with what might in other circumstances have been the beginnings of a migraine. A young couple joined him under the canopy but kept their distance, seeing and hearing only each other, like lovers everywhere, in any age. When a bus came at last they boarded but he stayed where he was, the fine rain slowly seeping into his clothing and moulding it to his body like a moist latex glove. Hours passed and more buses came and went but he did not move. There was no longer any point. Midnight came and dopplered into yesterday, bleaching out the shadows and dulling the lights.

Why won't they listen?

The exhausted blooms bound to the post told him why. Chrysanthemums and carnations, cheap and bought in a hurry. This was where he had fallen from grace; why he kept coming back to the same spot, repeating the pattern of that night over and over again. It was partly compulsion, but there was also a secret hope, that maybe this time it would end differently. But it never would because it never could. This was why he could never go home again, and why no one would listen to his anguish. One false step was all it had taken. He'd been drunk and foolish. His appetites had got the better of him and he strayed from the path, crossing the road without looking, intent only on chicken and chips. Straight in front of a bus. And there it was, the truth told in chrysanthemums and carnations, flowers in the rain.

Now, he was fading from his friends' attention as inexorably as he was fading from this night into the longer one, the unending dark. No one listens to the dead, except in memory. Sure, they'll talk about you now and then but it won't be for long, and never in the same way as when you were alive. They'll even talk *to* you, to ask you how and why; but they won't listen if you reply, just continue to think the worst. You're never really forgiven for dying, especially when you die of your own stupidity, or by your own hand. There is barely-concealed anger, a not-quite hidden sense of betrayal. You've hurt them and they want *closure*. When all is said and done, getting over loss means *forgetting*. For all the funeral suits and well-meant eulogies, for all the temporary tears and tributes, a thoughtless death unfriends you as swiftly and mercilessly as a mouse-click on Facebook. All you're left with is a bunch of fucking flowers, and pretty soon they're as dead and gone as you are.

Suspicious Minds

It's not every morning you wake up and find a stranger sitting naked and quite dead on your toilet. It was around half past five and I'd struggled out of bed because my bladder was in urgent need of emptying, thanks to the beer I'd put away the previous evening. I had to get up early anyway, though I really could have done with a good, long lie-in.

The guy was there when I switched on the light. Definitely a guy, as naked as the day he was born. Naturally, I thought he must have been some kind of hallucination brought on by insufficient sleep, anxiety and a surfeit of alcohol. I turned off the light, closed my eyes and rubbed them in the dark, took a deep breath and told myself to calm down. When I pressed the switch again he was still there. Not quite believing my own senses, I reached down and pressed two fingertips against his carotid artery. He was cold, blue-lipped and pallid, and nothing within his body was moving. I moved away, pissed in the hand basin, and turned the tap on to rinse it before washing my hands. Then I returned my attention to the dead man and looked at him more closely.

The corpse was slightly overweight, with thinning brown hair, a couple of days' growth of darker stubble speckling the lower part of his face. His eyes were closed and he looked peaceful, almost happy. I guessed he was around fifty, a once-handsome man gone to seed. His chest bore old scars, neat and precise, suggestive of cardiac surgery. My money was on a heart attack – a massive one, of course. They always are. I carefully took his hand and raised it easily. Chilly but no rigor mortis. His face didn't ring any bells at all.

Whoever he was, the dead man couldn't have been there long. I'd taken a leak before retiring at about one o'clock, about half an hour after getting home following a lengthy session at the pub. He hadn't been there when I hit the sack and I was pretty damned sure he wasn't anywhere else in my flat.

Backing out of the lavatory, I checked the rest of my home. The man had left no clothing lying around, and as far as I could see the doors and windows were as locked and bolted as they'd been when I went to bed. Indeed, everything was exactly as I remembered leaving it. My new suit and ironed shirt were still hanging on the wardrobe door and my wallet and other valuables were all present and undisturbed. He hadn't made himself tea, coffee or a sandwich before heading for my khazi and preparing to meet his maker. It seemed he'd simply turned up my flat, stark bollock naked, sat on the bog – and died. If he'd had a quiff and mirror shades he would have been the ultimate Elvis impersonator.

Somehow, that seemed appropriate. I'd always found

the manner of Presley's death strangely comforting. It was surely fitting that a king should die on the throne. But I drew the line at people dying on mine.

I returned to my bedroom and considered phoning the police. To be honest, I was in two minds about doing that. I had an important appointment later that morning, one I really didn't want to miss. The corpse would probably keep until it was all over, but if I left it sitting there I would only be storing up further complications. Besides, the last –and only – time I'd called them for assistance was a year before when I thought someone was breaking into the house across the road. They didn't turn up for nearly four hours, by which time the couple who lived there had been relieved of everything they had that was of any value and wasn't on them while they were away in Lanzarote. When a car with two coppers had arrived it was at a leisurely pace and one of them was still eating a bacon sandwich when they entered the property.

On the whole, I had little choice but to call 999. But, Sod's Law being what it is, I knew with utter certainty that if I called them before I was dressed they'd be here mob-handed with dogs and a firearms unit, and breaking down the door while I was still trying to get a second leg into my boxer shorts. Besides, the bloke on the bog wasn't going to be any less dead when they showed their faces, so I made myself presentable and put the kettle on before picking up the phone.

When the boys in blue came I was in my kitchen with a mug of coffee, a pack of painkillers and a cigarette. I'd left the door open so they wouldn't have the bother of knocking and waiting for me to let them in.

Disappointingly, there were only three of them – no adrenaline-fuelled action junkies with stubby machine-guns, no Alsatians or sniffer dogs – but I supposed that was just as well. My flat isn't very big and I hate crowds. I offered them coffee but there were no takers. However, I did find myself face down across the table and being handcuffed before I knew what was happening, with one of them pressing my face hard into the varnished pine surface. Meanwhile, two of them went to check out the stiff. The officer who'd cuffed me dragged me along in their wake. He wasn't exactly gentle about it.

'He's as dead as a fucking dodo,' said one as he gazed at the body. 'Looks like a kinky sex-game that went tragically wrong. Or maybe a drug overdose,' he added hopefully. 'Kinky sex-games and drugs.'

'Or maybe we've got ourselves another Denis Nielsen,' said the third, eyeing me speculatively. 'Kinky sex-games, drugs and murder. Killing for company and all that.'

'Is the victim anyone famous?' the handcuff man asked, presumably because he didn't want to be left out of the burgeoning fantasy. 'Kinky sex-games, drugs and murder, *and* a celebrity.'

'Nobody I recognise,' said the first. 'Mind you, I don't recognise any bloody celebrities nowadays. Not even with their clothes off.'

I gazed at each of them in turn. 'Officers,' I said. 'There were no kinky sex-games, no drugs and no murders. For one thing, I'm strictly heterosexual and my fiancée will vouch for that. For another, I've never seen that man before in my life. Or his. I have no idea who he is or what he's doing sitting on my bog starkers. All I know is that he's dead and he wasn't there when I went to bed at one this morning. I honestly don't know where he came from, how he got in, where his clothes are, or how he died.' I kept my diagnosis to myself. In my experience even the most open-minded police officers don't like you telling them how to do their job.

The first copper, who was a good few years older than the others and a sort of natural boss by dint of age and demeanour, squinted at me. 'Well, there are no signs of a forced entry. You must have let him in. It stands to reason.'

'Yeah,' said Handcuffs, his fevered imagination now unleashed. 'You let him in and had pervy sex, then you topped him. I expect you were jealous because he's famous and you're not. What did you use – knife, gun, blunt instrument?'

'There's not a bloody mark on him apart from those old scars,' I pointed out.

Handcuffs sneered. 'Drugs, then. Or poison. Or suffocation. Hey, that's it – auto-erotic asphyxiation gone wrong.'

'Hang on a minute, just now I killed him during a kinky sex game. Make up your mind.'

'That's what I said,' Handcuffs replied, puzzled. 'Auto-erotic asphyxiation gone wrong.'

'Auto-erotic asphyxiation only needs one person,' I said. 'Kinky sex games require at least two players.'

'So, you admit it,' Handcuffs growled. 'You're coming down to the station with us, chummy. Fucking nonce.'

I rolled my eyes. My big day was probably already ruined so there seemed no point in keeping my mouth shut any longer. 'Suit yourselves. I'm sure the post-mortem will show that he wasn't stabbed, shot, strangled, poisoned or beaten to death. And it will show that I didn't have sex with him before or even after he died. There will be no evidence to suggest that I committed any crime.'

Older Copper squinted at me again. 'So, a forensically-aware killer, eh? Well, you won't get away with this, you cocky little bastard. I'm arresting you on suspicion of murder. You do not have to say anything, but it may harm your defence if you do not mention when questioned something which you later rely on in court. Anything you do say may be given in evidence.'

The third copper, clearly bored with the banter, was examining the dead man's back. 'Here, look at this,' he suddenly remarked, taking the corpse by the shoulders and unceremoniously bending it forward.

'Shouldn't you be waiting for forensics before you start moving stuff around?' I asked, genuinely concerned about procedure but also beginning to get a bit worried that these clowns might decide to plant something incriminating on the body – perhaps even *in* it.

'Forensics,' said Older Copper disdainfully. 'Bunch of bloody kids, most of them. And they're all sodding civilians nowadays. What do they know about crime scenes and evidence?'

As he spoke, the corpse slowly toppled forward and fell in a sorry heap on my bathroom floor, face down and arse upward. The impact was surprisingly quiet. But it was revealing in more ways than one. 'Livor mortis,' I said as soon as I saw the rear view.

'What are you talking about?' said Handcuffs. 'He's completely bloody limp. Can't have been dead long.'

'No, that's rigor mortis you're thinking of. Livor mortis is the reddish-purple discolouration on his back and arse, and down the back of his legs. It's where the blood pools and coagulates after death. That and the body's flexibility tell me two things. Firstly, that he didn't die here. He's been moved post-mortem. Secondly, for livor mortis to show like that he must have been in one position – on his back – long enough for it to form. That indicates he was moved after rigor mortis dissipated. He's been dead at least fort-eight hours, perhaps as long as three, four days. No smell of decomposition so I'd say he's been kept chilled. And, he's perfectly clean. No mess on him or in or around the toilet bowl.'

Older Copper glared at me. 'And that means what exactly, smart-arse?'

I sighed. These three really were hard work. 'It means he was laid on his back almost immediately after death and was moved after rigor mortis had worn off,' I explained. '*Ergo*, the deceased did not die *in situ*. As for being washed, corpses tend to void bodily waste when their bladder and sphincter muscles slacken, so he must have been cleaned up some time after he died and before he was brought here.'

Handcuffs and Third Policeman stared at me, open-mouthed. 'How the fuck do you know so much about it?' Older Copper enquired, his brow furrowed in both annoyance and resentment.

'Well,' I replied modestly. 'I am, as you so astutely observed, forensically aware. I must also confess that I am quite well known to the police. And I now have a pretty good idea how that dead bloke got to be here.'

'I bloody knew it,' Older Copper crowed triumphantly.

I suspect he was barely able to see me through his visions of promotion, commendations and his grizzled picture in the papers. 'You've got form, haven't you?'

'Not exactly,' I responded, 'but your Major Incident Team know who I am. As it happens, I was out drinking with a few of them last night. And some of my colleagues.'

Handcuffs and Third Policemen gaped even wider. 'Christ,' said Handcuffs incredulously. 'Out on the piss with MIT while you had a body stashed in your bathroom? You've got some bleeding front, haven't you?'

'Not really. I'm a Home Office pathologist. I'm getting married later today. Last night was my stag do. Everyone was a bit pissed. My mates must have taken this body from the mortuary and sat him down on my toilet as a bit of a prank while I was asleep. Picking my lock must have been child's play to seasoned detectives. It shows imagination, I suppose. Makes a change from the usual handcuffing of the groom naked to a lamp-post.' I flexed my elbows ineffectually and smiled ruefully. 'Though it seems I didn't entirely escape the handcuffs, eh?'

Boracic Park

He couldn't take his eyes off it, so blue and purple and white against the mud and wispy grass that it was as if a small patch of summer evening sky had fallen to ground, flickering with a hint of silver like early stars. It seemed to suck the light into itself, making the surrounding area seem duller and dirtier than ever. Things of beauty were as rare as unicorn tears in this neck of the woods, and this was lovely almost beyond description. Most people would have walked the twenty feet or so that separated them and simply picked it up and taken it away, but he was powerless to move, mesmerised by its very presence. He was still gazing dreamily at it half an hour later when his girlfriend turned up.

'Kennedy, where the fuck have you been?' she slurred. The mixed fumes of Ace cider and Thunderbird might have suffocated a lesser mortal but it was all in a day's drunken idling to Kennedy. 'I've been looking all over for you. Has your giro come yet?' she added hopefully.

Scatty Mary wasn't really Kennedy's girlfriend, though when talking with other people he called her that because it was a convenient way of affirming a complex relationship without having to explain its peculiarities and nuances. Really, they were drinking buddies and accomplices rather than lovers, even if every once in a while, if they were both up for it and in a fit state, they engaged in clumsy, inexpert and largely unsatisfying sexual congress. Otherwise, they shared what they bought with their meagre benefits – food, smokes, booze and sometimes drugs, always the cheapest they could possibly find – teamed up for shoplifting sessions in the local supermarkets, joined forces against the scumbag kids who preyed on vulnerable people on their estate, and generally looked out for each other. By unspoken agreement, their relationship, such as it was, required no formal acknowledgement. Not that either of them would have dreamed of saying it.

'We don't get giros anymore, Mary,' he gently reminded her. 'The dosh goes straight into our bank accounts now, once a month on the dot. Pay day is tomorrow. Remember?'

Her eyes were fuzzy and her face blank. Not that Kennedy saw the condition she was in. He was still staring raptly at that tiny piece of heaven on earth. She shrugged, hiccupped, sagged against him 'I don't fucking know, do I?'

'That's why you go to the hole in the wall, woman. Barclays on the corner of the High Street. That's why I always stand next to you when we go there so those bastard kids don't rob you. The hole in the fucking wall.'

Mary laughed. 'Don't ask me. I'm so pissed I'm seeing double. Anyway, what's fucking wrong with you?'

'I think I'm hallucinating, Mary. I think I may have the fucking DTs. That or it's a religious experience, satori or something. I don't suppose you happen to have a drink on you?'

'On me? No, but I've got a bit *in* me. I went over to Sandra's place – that's Sandra with the kids, not Sandra with the job. She kicked her Brad out and he left some bottles behind, so she let me have a drink. There wasn't much left. Just enough for a quick swig. Well, a few.'

'Brad? Isn't that the bloke who looks like Idris Elba? Luther?'

'No, Brad's a white geezer. The one who looks like Luther's Sandra's brother.'

'Right. So why did she kick him out? Brad, not Luther.'

Mary looked furtively from left to right, checking to make sure no one was in earshot. 'Brad was giving that girl next door one, and he got her up the spout. Sandra went fucking ballistic.'

Still unable to tear his gaze from that gorgeous, ethereal patch of summer sky, Kennedy furrowed his brow in concentration. 'Hang on a minute, that Sandra – isn't she that sour-faced harridan who accused you of purloining her milk last week?'

'Yeah, that's her.'

'I'm surprised she let you through the door.'

'Oh, you know what they're like round here. She wanted to bend someone's ear about Brad. I just happened to be passing. Anyway, I did her a favour. That milk was fucking *off*. Anyway, who fucking cares? This sofa's just the job. Makes a change to have somewhere comfy to sit on a nice day. Got any fags?'

The sofa, a filthy, broken-backed and ripped two-seater that had been dragged from the nearest collection point for large refuse items and into the estate's grassy central square by a couple of enterprising youths inspired by *The Wire*, was only comfortable by default. It was that or the threadbare, rutted lawn. Exposed to the elements for nearly a month, it had only just dried out from a recent downpour that had caused it to bulge at the sides. It stank of mould, stale piss, stagnant water – and dog shit, courtesy of Kennedy, who had taken the trouble to smear canine excrement around the hole where he hid his most treasured possessions safe from the ferret-eyed child thugs who roamed the estate in small, semi-feral packs. Now, without looking but somehow taking great care to avoid touching the sides, he reached into the evil-smelling aperture and brought forth a battered tobacco tin. The words 'Old Holborn' were just about visible through the rust and dirt.

'Dog-ends only, I'm afraid. Roll it yourself. Matches are in there.'

Mary squinted at him. She was very drunk – and had spiced up the booze with a couple of diazepam tablets – and her vision was further hampered by the fact that she had long ago lost her spectacles and couldn't afford a new pair. She could barely see anything further than two yards away. 'Fucking look at me when you're talking to me,' she said, pouting. 'You can be so bleeding rude, Kennedy.'

At thirty-one years of age, at the arse-end of a life of poverty, hopelessness and serious over-indulgence, Scatty Mary was, frankly, past her best. Not that she'd ever been what a lot of men would call attractive. Plain was as good as it got for her – average, homely and unnoticed. At school the boys paid her little attention. Mary wasn't pretty enough to lust after, and not sufficiently ugly to be thought up for a mercy shag. She started drinking at seventeen, just to ease the boredom of unemployment and the loneliness of being perpetually ignored. At eighteen she had graduated to sporadically experimenting with the cheap drugs then flooding the town – skag, crack, sulphate and meth – and had begun what was to become a lifelong regime of prescription antidepressants and sleeping pills. The booze and medication, legal and otherwise, wore her down physically and exacerbated a naturally distracted and forgetful demeanour. Her lifestyle had taken its toll. Then, when she was twenty-five, along came Kennedy.

She squinted again, struggling to follow Kennedy's gaze at the same time as she was attempting to focus on rolling a cigarette using his dust-dry and semi-charred tobacco. 'Anyway, what the fuck *are* you staring at?'

Her comrade smiled blissfully. 'A vision of paradise, my dear. A tiny glimpse of the fucking divine.'

Unlike Mary, Kennedy was educated and experienced in the ways of the world beyond the estate. Twelve years her senior, he'd gone to a private school, had a degree of some sort from the London School of Economics, a former career in finance, a long-lost house in the suburbs. He was posh, or had been, once upon a time. Sometimes he spoke vaguely of a wife. Just as often he rambled on about his own culpability in his downfall. 'I had two good friends called Charlie,' he would say. 'I was so very fond of them. I spent all my money on them, and when that was not enough I spent the company's dosh. My very dear friends, the best pals a man could hope for. Oh, it wasn't just them. There were the horses and the women, and the casinos and the poker. But it was Charlie and Charlie that did the damage. Champagne and cocaine totally buggered my judgement and I was caught with my hands in the till. Up to the fucking elbows, they were. Christ, no wonder she told me to sling my fucking hook. The Blessed Virgin might forgive me, but *she* never will.' Kennedy was also a Catholic, but Scatty Mary didn't mind. God was a concept that hove into view only when she was in trouble.

'What, can you see angels or something?' Mary continued to squint but all she could see was a patchwork blur that she knew were grimy windows, council concrete and something that used to be a grassed square, though everyone on the estate called it 'the park' – perhaps because the kids sometimes played desultory and disorganised games of football there, until the cheap plastic balls punctured and they returned to the telly and loitering outside the offie, or went off to mug someone.

Kennedy laughed. 'Better than that. I can see salvation, Mary – *salvation*. They say the Lord moves in mysterious ways, his wonders to perform – and this is *really* mysterious. In fact, around here it's a fucking miracle, plain and simple. Tell me, Mary – what is the best thing that could happen to you right now? I mean, right at this very minute?'

She hiccupped, then coughed. 'A proper fag would be nice, with fresh baccy instead of this manky shit we have to smoke, other people's poxy old dog-ends. And a decent drink. Cider. They're doing two-litre bottles of Taurus Dry for £1.99 in Aldi. Oh, and one of those doughnuts with custard in. I haven't eaten a thing all day. Been saving my money for tonight.'

'And now, Mary,' Kennedy asked, still staring blissfully into a distance Mary could not discern, 'how much of Her Majesty's sterling do you actually have at your disposal at this time?'

'Fifty-two pence, in coppers. I though we could, you know, pool our resources, as you always say.'

'Indeed I do, and indeed we shall. And at this moment I have precisely one pound and five pence in my pocket – what they used to call a guinea, I believe. I too am dying for a smoke of quality, a fine beverage, and victuals. But we are not going to get very far with £1.57, are we? We couldn't even get a can of gnat's piss and a packet of crisps with that.' He laughed again.

'Yeah, alright, so we're skint,' she said morosely. 'Totally fucking boracic. I dunno why you're so bleeding happy about it. Our giros don't come until tomorrow. What are we gonna do until then?'

'I told you, Mary – no giros anymore. We're on our own until Barclays' mechanical minions cough up our funds in the morning.'

'I suppose we could do a spot of thieving,' Mary said half-heartedly.

'I don't think so. I'm getting too bloody old and arthritic for that shit,' said Kennedy. 'Manual dexterity has deserted me. Remember that last time in Sainsbury's? I dropped that bottle of gin because I couldn't get it down my trousers before the security guard saw me. I'm too old, too slow and too knackered for shoplifting. A fucking dinosaur.' He chuckled. 'But all is not lost. Today the saints have smiled upon us.' He rose unsteadily from the sofa and walked carefully forward.

Mary watched until he merged with the background and became, to her failing eyes, invisible. Suddenly, she became afraid. What if he really did disappear? What if he never came back from that sea of swimming, inconstant outlines and unfathomable, shifting blocks of grey and brown? What would she do without him? Her friends were not exactly friends, she knew that. Kennedy was the only person on the estate who didn't call her Scatty Mary to her face. He was the only one who'd never lied to her or tried to cheat her in some way. Whatever he had, he shared it with her. She was always made welcome in his tiny, one-bedroom flat, allowing her the run of it. He'd never shouted at her, or hit her, or insulted her. He looked after her, made her feel safe, kept her away from the bad drugs. And...

She choked back an unexpected and uncharacteristic sob. 'Please come back,' she whispered.

Gradually, he emerged from the formless chaos her short-sightedness made of the estate. When he got closer, she saw that he was grinning widely, his usually pale face flushed beneath the untidy brown hair. She'd forgotten he was so tall, that his fingers – piano fingers, her mother would have said – were so long. Those fingers were clutching something rectangular and a kind of bluish-purple colour with a hint of white, a flash of silver.

'What have you got?'

'Well, I thought I was seeing things, because it honestly isn't the sort of thing people like me see, and certainly not in these parts. I had to convince myself that it was real. And it was you that did it, Mary. Talking to you made me sure I wasn't fucking dreaming. So I went over to claim squatter's rights, and here it is. Would you like to hold it?'

She cupped and held out her hands, and Kennedy solemnly placed a crisp, fresh £20 note in between them.

Mary gasped, held it reverently up to the light, sniffed at it, then gave it back to him. She rummaged in her trouser pocket and offered him a handful of coppers, which he accepted with a smile.

'That's £21.57 in the kitty, Mary. That should be enough for a medium-sized packet of Golden Virginia, eight litres of Taurus Dry, and a few doughnuts, if we shop wisely. I fancy a chocolate one. We'll go back to my place when we've got them. There's an old episode of *Lovejoy* on the Drama channel later. And after that...' Kennedy waggled his eyebrows suggestively and offered her his arm. She rose unsteadily and took it, and they set off across the park for the nearest Aldi, which was handily placed right next to the bank.

As they walked, Mary began to fret. 'Don't you feel a bit, you know, guilty about taking that money? It might belong to some really poor person, a pensioner or something.'

'Not at all,' said Kennedy confidently. 'For one thing, poor people rarely lose money. They don't dare to. So they take good care of it, no matter what. When was the last time you lost any money, even a couple of pence?'

Mary thought about it. 'I don't think I ever have,' she said wonderingly. 'Maybe the odd penny when I was a kid and money didn't seem to matter, but definitely not since I left home and had to fend for myself.'

'There you go,' he said. 'The poor hang on to what they've got for as long as possible. Pensioners only lose money if somebody steals it, and thieves guard their takings jealously. Only rich people care so little about money that they don't take good care of it. I didn't when I had plenty of cash, until the two Charlies came along and made me both stupid and unacceptably careless. But now, like you, I am poor. I don't lose money. I share what I have with you, but I never fucking *lose* it.'

Mary sighed contentedly and pressed against him, causing them both to stumble. 'And I share what I have with you,' she said when they'd regained their balance. 'You're a good man, Kennedy. You're always nice to me, and you always treat me well.'

'Well, of course I do,' Kennedy replied, stooping to perfunctorily kiss her cheek. 'Of course I do. What do we have if we don't have each other?'

Before Tomorrow

We all put off until tomorrow that which should really be done today, and in that respect he was no different to anyone else. His life was a long parade of undone things that, many years before, were definitely going to be addressed on that illusory next day: the girl he was going to phone, now a middle-aged lady married to someone else; the book he was going to start writing, now long-forgotten; that trip to New York; all those thousand and one items on his 'bucket list'. Now the bucket was fast approaching and tomorrow was as far off as it ever had been. The list was no shorter.

Sterling sat in his comfortable armchair and sipped Earl Grey tea from a bone china cup. Liquid had slopped into the saucer so he had to take care not to get drips on his shirt, fresh from the wardrobe and still reeking of camphor and fabric conditioner, courtesy of the painstaking Mrs Whitby. He wasn't keen on aromatic chemicals but one of his few daily pleasures was the gradual replacement of those odours with the smell of cigar smoke and his own gin-scented sweat as the day wore on. It was, he reflected, a bit sad really. But he supposed lonely old bachelors had to take what they could get. Time had whittled away at his friends until there were few of them left, and most of those too decrepit to do more than pick up the telephone occasionally. The weekly nights out at the pub had become monthly, quarterly, and eventually annual affairs, with each one likely to be the valedictory appearance of at least one of their number. Intimate feminine companionship was non-existent – even ladies of a certain age no longer found him even remotely appealing, and he was too proud to resort to paying for the company of women. It was probably for the best, as he strongly doubted his ability to perform to even his own satisfaction.

The pain in his abdomen was getting worse with each day that passed. He knew what it was, of course. The oncologist had been forthright and pessimistic. Soon enough he would have no *mañana* to look forward to. Upstairs, in the bathroom cabinet, there was morphine; but the pain was not yet bad enough for that. Until it was he would self-medicate with gin and tonic, brandy and vintage port. And his cigars, naturally. One of the few perks of being old and single was being able to fumigate the place as and when he wished. Oh, there was his visiting housekeeper, Mrs Whitby, who could often be heard muttering to herself when he was enjoying one of his 2002 vintage Cohibas, but she didn't complain too vociferously. He paid her very well, and she was bright enough to know better than to fall out with her meal-ticket. Actually, Sterling paid her too well, he knew; but she did a good job and didn't try to take the place over like some of his previous employees. Besides, she was a bit of company, and touchingly loyal in her own way. He wondered briefly if he should tell her that he was dying, but dismissed the thought. That could wait. So could changing his will. He still had a bit more time – several months, probably. Maybe a year, but certainly no more.

What had her name been? Janet? Janice? Janine? He smiled at the absurdity. He'd been in love with the woman but now he couldn't remember her name. Yet he could see her face clearly in his mind's eye. Come to think of it, there was a photograph of her in an album upstairs, with her name written on the back. Perhaps he would look at it later. Jeanette? No, not that, not quite.

She'd moved to the Midlands to care for her ailing grandfather, so she'd said. Sterling hadn't been entirely convinced. An insecure youth, he'd suspected that it was just the excuse she needed to get away from him, an *adieu* disguised as an *au revoir*. The affection she'd shown him had always felt too good to be true and he'd resigned himself to losing her sooner or later. She'd phoned him shortly after, from Wolverhampton or Walsall or wherever – a halting, awkward conversation memorable only for its banality and his sense that she was disappointed in his hurt, laconic responses – and he'd promised to call her back in a few days that had somehow stretched into nearly thirty years. There had always been time and then there wasn't. Then it didn't matter anymore. Years later he'd heard from a mutual friend that she'd married, had children. That had hurt, but not as much as it would once have done.

There had been no one else. Dalliances and flings, yes; but they were mere entertainments. There had been nothing serious or lasting. He'd always assumed that one day he would meet someone else he cared as much about but it had never happened. Sterling didn't need to wonder why. There was no need for introspection. He was well aware that he'd had his chance and, as they said nowadays, blown it.

It was the same with his career. Decades spent in middle management because he never felt quite ready for promotion. He was young and professional advancement, like so many other things, could wait. Then suddenly youth had gone and the time had fled in its wake. Retirement brought a windfall, a lump sum payment and a decent pension. There was money from his late parents' properties, an inheritance from an uncle – another solitary bachelor with an apparently empty past – so he wasn't poor. He could afford his luxuries, the booze and cigars, the cinema and theatre, and Mrs Whitby. But he'd achieved nothing of note or worth. In his former workplace he was forgotten. To distant relatives he was only a name in a genealogy. Until lately he had no one he wanted to leave anything to. It wouldn't be long before he would be nothing but scattered entries in official records. Cremation wouldn't even leave a plot of ground and a headstone to mark his passing.

The clock on the mantelpiece chimed eleven o'clock. Sterling rose and made for the drinks cabinet. A very large G&T was required. The sun must surely be over the bloody yard-arm somewhere on the planet and he needed something to quell the growing ache in his guts. And that deeper ache, the one that comes with the realisation that a stroll down memory lane is a solitary walk along an empty street scheduled for demolition.

The drink needed ice and lemon but Mrs Whitby was

cleaning the kitchen and she would frown upon his drinking so early in the day. The liquid was warm and bitter on his tongue. On an empty stomach it would go to his head fairly quickly. Good. He drained the glass and made himself another, sipping this one more slowly as he stood gazing into a distance that wasn't anywhere that could be seen in the street outside his window.

Yes, it does, he thought suddenly. *It does matter and it always did.*

Mrs Whitby would be surprised to learn that she was to be the sole beneficiary of his estate. Sterling knew she had two daughters with young children of their own, and that they struggled to make ends meet. Mrs Whitby wouldn't need any advice on what to do with the money. A million pounds wasn't as substantial a sum as it had been in his youth but it would still make several lives more pleasant. And who else could he leave it to? Charities that would absorb it effortlessly in CEO salaries and PR consultants? Distant relatives who barely knew he existed and didn't care one way or the other? His few remaining friends, who would all be in his position in the near future and would face the same dilemma? No, this way he would be able to make a real difference to the lives of a few people. And who could tell? One day one of Mrs Whitby's grandchildren might do something wonderful and of lasting benefit to humanity thanks to the start he had given them. Or they might fritter the lot away on drink and drugs, half-arsed get-rich-quick schemes and flashy cars. Well, he'd be dead and gone and it would be their money and their choice. Everyone had to make their own mistakes and learn from them if they could.

He never had. And now it did matter. It mattered a great deal. The bucket-list was always a pipe-dream, but surely he could have crossed off a few items as he waited for the right moment for others? New York would never happen now. Nor would the Great Pyramid, the Grand Canyon, Ayers Rock, the Northern Lights, the Great Wall of China, the Acropolis, Machu Picchu, Niagara Falls…

Not even the bloody Eiffel Tower. Where had all those tomorrows gone?

He returned to the drinks cabinet and splashed more gin into the glass. The spirit had indeed gone to his head and now he was in the mood for more. Mrs Whitby's disapproval didn't count for much when set against everything else, all those things he had never seen or touched, and the darkness and silence fast approaching. Anyway, what business was it of hers? She was paid to clean, do his shopping and laundry, and prepare his meals, not to advise him on health matters or correct his behaviour. Mrs Whitby wasn't a friend or counsellor, only an employee, his retirement luxury.

Janette. The sudden recollection sobered him. Her name was Janette. Sterling didn't even bother with the Schweppes but tipped the gin straight down his throat, barely registering the taste. She had been lovely, sweet-natured and vibrant – so much life in such a small frame that he had been almost unable to believe that she was real. And he'd never been able to believe that she could be his. Janette Marker. What would have happened if he had made that telephone call? Would they have stayed together? Would they have been happy? Would there have been children, trips to those places he had once so longed to see?

The photograph upstairs was the only surviving memento of their time together. Yet he had only looked at it once or twice in all the years since. He had never been one for looking back because his past was as disappointing as the future was empty. *What might have been could never have existed.* He'd read that somewhere years before and it had struck a chord. It was one of the few quotations he'd ever bothered to commit to memory. He hadn't really understood why at the time, but he had come to understand. It was his epitaph. His whole life was composed of might-have-beens. He may as well never have existed.

Sterling stared absently into the now-empty glass then placed it on the mantelpiece next to the clock. Why was it still ticking? What was the point of those hands chasing each other round the dial when all that awaited him was as blank and bereft of purpose as what had gone before? The realisation sickened him. The sensation was accompanied by a brief but terrible pain deep in his guts and he bent forward, his hands gripping his thighs tightly. Sterling momentarily considered the morphine but the agony quickly subsided. He knew that soon enough it would be constant; and that would only cease when everything else did.

For the first time since he was a young man, he felt a sense of urgency. The will needed to be finalised and signed. He reached for the telephone and called his solicitor to make an appointment for that afternoon. Then he asked Mrs Whitby to join him in the lounge so that he could give her the good news and the bad. After that there would be the small matter of attempting to trace the former Miss

Janette Marker, just to say hello and, inevitably, goodbye; just to let her know that he remembered.

There was so much to do before tomorrow.

Pyromancer

It blossoms outward in slow motion, an expanding yellow-orange tongue that warps and dissolves whatever it licks. Curtains and wallpaper shrivel and curl, carpet and upholstery crisp and crumble into soot, sucked upward and blindly along as the heat urgently seeks exit. Glass shatters, bursting into the street like hot, sharp tears from eyes angry with flame. Someone inside is screaming but the sound is soon drowned by approaching sirens. When the emergency services arrive and their mechanical noise ceases, there is nothing left to hear but the crackle and roar of burning, muted asides from a growing crowd of onlookers, terse exchanges between the uniforms, then the hiss of water on hot ash as the hoses begin to play across the scorched façade.

This is not his first and it will not be the last. He bears witness from a broken window in a tenement stairwell nearby. He can feel the heat even at this range. He tastes the smoke, with its tang of accelerant and hint of cooked meat. He hears the flame performing its task as planned. He listens to its message, the voice of burning flesh and wood, cloth and plastic, the shouted interjections of the crowd and the firefighters, the fading echoes of that scream.

The fire speaks. It says

this is all there is

He nods, satisfied. The wind picks up and more smoke billows across his face and into his lungs. He coughs, and the spasm fuels his euphoria. As usual, he has an erection; and as always, he embraces the arousal and eagerly rides it to its crescendo, confident that there will be no interruption. He is unseen. All eyes are on the conflagration, all attention focused on his work.

Minutes later, the space he occupies in the stairwell is vacant. The only traces of his presence, the only evidence that he was ever there, are little pools of pearly fluid on a tiled floor that has seen more than its share of such emissions; a charred shell of a house; and a roasted corpse. And the blue lights flashing and the spectators whispering and the water glistening, falling sapphire droplets in the steady rhythm of the lights.

This was not the first and it will not be the last. His hands are acrid with petrol, the hairs singed away, small burns on his fingers. A thin layer of soot coats his face. The smoke is settled tightly in his lungs, dissolving in mucus – a thick soup of carcinogens cooking in his chest. He doesn't care. Death is a fire, and he knows he will one day burn. The manner of his passing means nothing. The time he has left means nothing. He yearns for the crematorium.

What is life anyway? It is an unending round of futile activity, a circle that only repeats and never changes. Living to work to pay to live; being in service for the right to eat and drink and breathe, for empty entertainment if there is anything left after the bills have been paid and impossible budgets conjured up to make ends meet until the next payday, when the cycle will begin again. A drink or a drug to make the time disappear, maybe a desperate fumble and a half-hearted shag if he is sufficiently off his head to have the inclination to pull and enough energy to get it up, something to regret when day breaks and he wakes to see a strange, unwanted head on the pillow next to him – someone whose disappointment will match his own when she opens her eyes and looks into his.

There are no goals. His life has no meaning, no purpose.

Except for the fire.

He walks aimlessly away into the night and the emptiness. No one sees him because there is nothing to see. He is only visible when the buildings burn and can only be heard when the occupants scream. Now the flames are dampened and the furnace is cooling. Evacuees from adjacent flats remain in a small cluster just outside the cordon, waiting for someone to tell them what to do. Dark flakes of ash rain slowly down around them and the casual spectators who begin to drift away to their homes in the surrounding estate, the adrenaline absorbed and processed and gone. He joins their exodus, sniffing deeply as they pass him on the way to their homes. Like him, they stink of smoke and their eyes are red from it, their cheeks and clothing spotted with it. It clogs their noses and deadens their olfactory senses. Like him, they are low-paid drones in the city hive, cheaply dressed and craving distraction from eternal boredom. He blends in. It is always this way. Even if they could see him they would not know him for what he was. Because in so many ways he is like them.

Yet he is different. When he was a boy, his older brother described the pictures he could see in the fireplace of their home – the glowing coals formed fantastic cities with minarets and spires, landscapes filled with dragons and salamanders, grotesque faces that appeared and dissolved as the fuel was consumed. He saw none of that. And he felt cheated. Then, one winter evening when the coal was banked high and he stared as the flames lapped and caught at each shiny black lump, he heard the fire speak. Its crackling whisper spoke to him alone, telling him the secret of his life, how to measure his time in ashes and embers. He listened and understood. Starting with dustbins and heaps of rubbish, moving on to garden sheds and unattended cars, then empty flats and derelict houses, he fed the fire and the fire nourished him. One day, a house turned out not to be as uninhabited as he'd thought.

The fire was pleased, its voice exultant, louder and clearer than ever before, a shout of boundless joy that lifted him to the threshold of orgasm and invited him to take himself across.

It said

I am what I am and I am all there is

Now he is its servant, its priest. Its lover.

The flat is cold and dark but he doesn't switch the lights on. He knows where everything is. He doesn't need to see. In the little kitchen he strips naked and puts everything – jacket, jeans, trainers, shirt, underwear – into the washing machine, adding detergent and selecting the fast cycle. He pads into the shower and turns the water to the hottest setting. When the water is scalding he lathers himself with shampoo and shower gel, gasping as his body itches with the heat. It is how he imagines it feels to burn alive – though he knows perfectly well that death by fire isn't like that at all. He coughs hard, hawks up sooty phlegm and spits it at his feet. He opens his eyes and allows the shampoo to sting them. He scrubs fiercely at his skin, rubs his scalp hard, scratching deep. Rinsing is so painful it is almost a pleasure.

It's an established routine now. He shuts off the water and stands in the shower stall, dripping wet, shivering and erupting in goosebumps in a chill he no longer feels. There is a towel on a hook on the inside of the door but he ignores it. There is no point in drying himself. He stays there for an age, immobile, not wanting to eat or drink, knowing he will not sleep for hours. He has no interest in television or books or music. It's too late now to go out, even if there was anywhere he wanted to be. The fire has been washed away and he is alone and empty once more. The future is a long, dismal corridor and at the end of it there is only flame.

He is a nobody. He is going nowhere. What little he owns is not worth having. But he has listened to the voice of the fire.

It said
there is nothing else

Imago

It seems to hang motionless for an instant, caught midway between her eyes and the candle burning at the other end of the bath. Then it darts in a jagged spiral, wings beating so fast the flame twitches in their draught, a tightening, uneven orbit that will surely end in destruction. If she moves, if she acts quickly, she could save the moth. All she has to do is sit up and bend forward to extinguish the candle with a breath or a wet, soapy finger. But she doesn't move. She watches in listless fascination as the insect rushes erratically to its undoubted end.

But at the last moment it tears itself free of the candle's spell and alights upon the tiled bathroom wall, settling so now she can clearly see the skull marked on its back. She relaxes, inhales the scent arising from aromatic bath oils and melting wax: jasmine and dewberry, sandalwood; cloying, almost comforting. But she doesn't take her eyes from the moth, the black, gold-speckled wings folded and stark against the white tile; the death's head, an omen of misfortune – a living *memento mori* crawling purposelessly across the glaze.

She remembers this moth from her older brother, an entomology bore whose impromptu lectures sometimes took root. This particular one had fascinated her, perhaps because of the creature's macabre beauty, and she'd paid close attention. *Acherontia atropos*. She smiles, appreciating the synchronicity. The moth is named for one of the rivers bordering the mythical Greek underworld, and for one of the Fates – Atropos, the one who cuts the thread of life to end it. She sighs and runs slippery wet hands over her face.

'My name is Moira,' she tells the moth. 'I know why you're here, Atropos. Is it done? Is it spun?'

She laughs at her own fancy. By the bath is an occasional table bearing a large glass of red wine. Without looking, she takes the glass in her left hand, brings it to her lips and drinks deeply, then stares into the blood-red liquid. Château Margaux, a 1994 vintage Bordeaux she's been saving for a special occasion – and they didn't come any more special than this.

Lifting one leg from the foamy water, she holds it straight at a forty-degree angle, examining it critically. Not a bad shape for her age, still slim and unblemished. The gleaming skin looks soft and deceptively smooth, though it's hard to tell in the dim light and with the best part of a bottle of wine inside her. She frowns, wondering why she made a point of laying the razor on the side of the bath before turning on the tap and adding oils and bubble bath to the steaming torrent. Then she remembers and is sad again. Dutch courage is essential but she mustn't let the inevitable *vin rouge* glow distract her from the business at hand. Or dull the pain. Right now she needs to feel the pain.

'Don't you agree, Atropos?' The moth has moved several tiles in a ten o'clock direction while she wasn't looking, but is still once more. 'No point cutting the thread if I don't feel the pain. Better stop drinking.' But she drains the glass anyway. 'He was perfect,' she says to her uncaring insect guest. 'Just what I always wanted. The kind of man I always dreamed of. Ticked all the boxes.'

The moth turns a hundred and eighty degrees and returns to the exact place it landed after its whirlwind flight around the candle. It stops moving. She watches it carefully. The life cycle of the lepidoptera, she recalls, is a four-stage progression: embryo, larva, pupa, imago. Egg, caterpillar, chrysalis, and butterfly or moth. *Acherontia atropos* usually lays her eggs on leaves of the Solanaceae family of plants, particularly *Atropa belladonna*, deadly nightshade. Atropos again, toxic and hallucinogenic – the beautiful bestower of deadly dreams. Having fed voraciously throughout its short existence, the infant creature coats itself with a kind of saliva that hardens the soft outer flesh into a tough shell, red as congealing blood, red as wine. Inside the shell the caterpillar's body undergoes an extreme metamorphosis, dissolving itself with its own juices and rearranging the tissues into its adult form.

'That's what he did to me,' she confides to the steamy, scented air. 'I was a happy caterpillar until I met him, munching my way through life without a care in the world, biding my time until he came along. He gutted me, turned me inside out. All I've done for the past few weeks is sit inside my little shell and hurt.'

Abruptly, the moth spreads its wings and launches

itself from the wall and toward the ceiling, fluttering in a drunkard's circle. 'Did it hurt when you were in your shell, Atropos?' she wonders aloud as it traces its crazy path through the air above her.

She turns on a tap, adding more hot water to the tub. Steam rises and falls. The change in temperature affects the convection currents in the bathroom's subtropical microclimate. The moth gains height as the steam rises, falls again when it meets a cooler stream, those gilded sable wings beating and beating. Wisps of vapour escape through the open transom, the moth's door, though the insect stubbornly refuses to exit, focused wholly on the candle flame.

She gasps as the bathwater becomes just a degree too hot for comfort. Her skin feels raw, her arms and legs tingle. Beneath the lather and water she is sweating. The man's face comes unbidden to her mind's eye. 'Bastard.' Her eyes prickle with the threat of tears but she's past all that and they do not fall. She's done her weeping. No more of that.

The razor is in her hand now, glinting in the candlelight. Expressionless, she studies the chrome handle, the thin slice of blade protruding from the head, turns it round to see an identical sliver of metal on the other side. A twist of the handle and the head opens like butterfly wings to reveal the Gillette blade seated snugly within. Another twist, and it closes. Open, close. It is so easy.

So easy. The moth has descended, spiralling around the candle once more, its little wings beating furiously, flashing orange and black. Open, close. She imagines it screaming as it nears the flame, a kamikaze pilot having second thoughts a fraction of a second too late. She closes her eyes and wishes she had more wine. But she has the dim lighting, the hot water, the heady mixture of scents, the razor. They will do for now.

'Bastard.'

Open, close. Open, close. Open.

She hears a brief hiss and an unexpected squeak. A smell of burning, something organic, a stench like singed hair, cuts momentarily through the other scents and is gone. The fluttering noise has ceased. Eyes still tightly shut, she places the razor against her skin. Her hand moves, swiftly and decisively. Then she does it again.

The scorched, dead moth floats in the bath. The water is still warm but the level has dropped several inches. The candle has burned down almost to the holder and the flame is guttering, dying. The razor lies abandoned on the table, next to the empty glass.

Two walls away, a landing and two doors away, she admires herself in the full-length mirror. 'Not bad for a woman my age,' she tells her reflection. The little black dress glitters with scattered constellations of tiny gold sequins. She's wearing black stiletto-heeled Jimmy Choos. The black stockings are wrinkle-free. She grins to herself as she recalls how easily they unrolled along her freshly shaven legs, how sensual it felt. The lipstick grin is as red as wine, as red as blood. Her hair falls across her shoulders like folded dark wings. It's exactly the effect she was aiming for, classy yet somehow understated, sexy without being tarty. She feels very grown up, a rare experience even though she is a year the wrong side of forty. 'You're a beautiful lady,' she says, as she's told herself so often before; and for once she means it.

The bedside clock says it is almost eight. He will be here soon, the new man, to take her to dinner, then a nightclub, then… Well, who can tell what will happen after that? Fate will take its course. Whatever happens, this man will take her mind off the last one, if only for a while. That will be time enough, and if she's lucky the short term could turn into the long haul. She laughs to herself and adds the finishing touch, her lucky earrings, black star diopside set in gleaming silver. 'No matter how much it hurts, if you fall off a horse, the best thing is to get straight back on.' She grins again, feeling wicked and seductive. Practice makes perfect.

She remembers that she hasn't emptied the bath, so she returns to the scene of her long soak and pulls the plug. Seeing the remains of the moth as it is slowly drawn toward the drain, she feels sad again, but only for an instant because the doorbell rings. He is here. 'Go get him, Moira,' she whispers.

She makes a quick detour for one last, nervous glance in the mirror before she reaches the door. To her horror, there's an inch of loose cotton thread sticking out from the neckline of her dress. How did she miss that? A little too much wine, maybe? She frowns and shrugs and decides she doesn't care if she is a tiny bit drunk, then reaches over to the dressing table for her nail scissors.

Haunted House

The once-famous but now unfashionable writer moved in on a sunny morning in late May. This, he thought as he delightedly explored the property on that first day, was the place he had been seeking for what seemed like forever – somewhere he could really *write*.

The rambling old house stood where a dense forest almost met the lake shore, far from any other dwelling, accessible only by an unpaved, unlit road that wasn't marked on any map. It had no history worth relating, only the happiness and fulfilment of its former occupants, ordinary people who would be fondly remembered but never celebrated outside their families. When the writer investigated the light, airy attic rooms all he found was a thin layer of dust and the memory of mice; the cellar was clean and dry, and contained only a worn broom, an empty bucket and a couple of meandering beetles.

The electrics and plumbing worked just fine. Lights did not flicker or fail, doors did not creak eerily or ominously refuse to budge when he tried them, windows opened and closed freely and only when required. Nothing unpleasant came out of the kitchen and bathroom taps, only clean water. There were no mysterious, decaying structures or disquieting earthen mounds in the gardens – no concealed wells, stagnant ponds or unexpected sinkholes. Nights were quiet and calm; the summer days were long, warm and comfortable. The neighbours left him alone – indeed, no one came by at all. The telephone never rang and he made no calls.

At the edge of the garden, the land fell a dozen or so feet down to a narrow strand separating his new home from the lake. Each day, for twenty or thirty minutes at dawn and dusk, he strolled aimlessly along that little beach, enjoying the birdsong, gathering his thoughts, looking across the waters at the low hills on the other side, the lights of the village nestling, barely visible, in a distant bay. Now and then he would wonder who lived there, what their lives were like. But that was rare. Mostly he simply basked in the twilight ambience, focused wholly on that expanding text. It was the only thing on his mind and the outside world was not permitted to encroach.

He spent nearly six months there in peaceful solitude, writing a new novel, a gothic horror story of tormented ghosts and an ancient, lurking evil, supernatural retribution that continued beyond the grave, redemption through love and self-sacrifice. In all that time, as his imagination caught fire and the story took shape, the only events of note were occasional visits to the garden by squirrels, badgers and foxes. Sometimes it rained lightly. Undisturbed and absorbed, he worked hard. His novel grew, was revised and polished.

At the end of October, the book was finished. He read through it one last time and nodded, satisfied. Everything about it was just right. It had turned out exactly as he'd envisaged. Now he could rest, though it was a shame the story would never be published. It was the best thing he'd ever done, far superior to anything he'd written while he was alive.

The Netherwold Heritage

When Victor Netherwold's last surviving relative died, at first he was very upset. Although since his late teens he hadn't been particularly close to his eccentric and secretive Uncle Vortigern – contact reduced to Christmas and birthday cards; an annual, grudgingly allowed visit to the old boy's large, rambling house across town in late summer, undertaken with a degree of trepidation; infrequent telephone calls – Victor had, in spite of everything, liked the old man and felt they'd got on quite well. Now he was forced to shoulder the burden of being the sole remaining representative of the family line.

And probably the end of it. At the age of thirty-nine, a decidedly homely and non-euphemistic confirmed bachelor on a low income, Victor's chances of reproducing were fairly slender. Normally, he didn't mind that at all. Free from domestic ties and responsibilities, he was able to indulge his interests without spousal interference or disapproval. In the main, that meant watching DVDs and sport on television, reading crime fiction, exploring whatever free entertainments London had to offer, and easing his loneliness with the aid of an extensive collection of mildly pornographic magazines. Family, he had long ago determined, from close observation of his parents' fractious relationship and his friends' squabbling siblings, was something best avoided. Yet the thought of being the only Netherwold in the entire city, if not the whole of Great Britain, made him dreadfully sad. He mourned his uncle, sincerely if not whole-heartedly.

The letter from his late uncle's solicitor was a real eye-opener. Uncle Vortigern left a sizeable portfolio of property, stocks and shares, and an eight-digit bank balance. When Victor realised that he was heir to all this – along with that enormous house and its entire contents – his sadness subsided somewhat. He could now move out of his tiny rented flat and give up work. No more getting out of bed at five in the morning to get ready for a long day of monotony in that print shop. No more struggling to make ends meet. Now he could devote all his time and energy to his preferred leisure pursuits. He might even take up another hobby. Perhaps he could learn to play guitar, or even the piano. Maybe he would travel to all those exotic holiday destinations his colleagues and few friends bafflingly always seemed able to afford. The world was his oyster, and it was no longer bounded by the M25.

Victor wondered if he should tweak his image to match his new status as a man of means. With that kind of money he would probably – at long last – have women throwing themselves at him. He might even lose his virginity. Yet wealth alone surely wouldn't be enough. Even the least scrupulous gold-digger would baulk at sleeping with an unattractive scruff like him. A new hairstyle? The comb-over was, he realised, little more than the memorial for a battle in which baldness had long ago triumphed over pointless vanity. It was definitely time for a change in the tonsorial department. The hedge-like eyebrows could also do with a trim. But radical surgery would be required to temper the over-large ears and the too-snub nose, and to bolster the weak chin. It was too early to think about that sort of thing. On the other hand, a wardrobe make-over was long overdue. He was still wearing some of his father's old clothes, for crying out loud. The workplace was one thing, any old rags would do for that – and he wasn't expected to dress up for his local pub, where all that counted among his fellow regulars were getting your round in and not being a complete disaster at the oche. But now he had expectations, perhaps even of a social life beyond the Black Horse, and rubbing shoulders with the wealthy required *fashion*. The threadbare 1970s suits and kipper ties, the shirts with long, pointed collars, the flared trousers – especially the flared trousers – they had to go, and that was that. The hand-me-downs had saved him a lot of money over the years, but now there was no need for thrift.

All that could wait until he'd taken possession of the house and the cash was safely salted away in his own bank account. When that was done, when he'd finished unloading his possessions from the removal van he'd yet to arrange, then he would have a bit of a spending spree. First, though, he had a funeral to attend.

It was practically a mansion. The spacious hall boasted a door on either side and another at the end, tucked beneath the arch of the wide staircase. The casual visitor might have been put off by the door knocker – a rusty iron skull that rapped against matching cross-bones – but the curios in that antechamber had been known to put even the most devoted Jehovah's Witness to flight. And Uncle Vortigern had always invited purveyors of religion into his home, on the pretext of desiring to learn whatever brand of spiritual bullshit was on offer. Then he would enjoy the fun.

To the right, there was a full length mirror in an ornate mahogany frame which on closer inspection turned out to be a scrimshaw lattice of finely-carved human figures engaged in the full range of sexual positions from the *Kama Sutra*, plus quite a few Vatsyayana and his sources had never imagined. Opposite that was a life-sized waxwork of Bela Lugosi as Dracula. Many an unsuspecting visitor had paused to inspect their appearance in the mirror, only to find the Count leering over their shoulder with fangs bared and marble eyes glittering evilly in the crimson lighting. The looming Transylvanian didn't deter Victor from admiring his new look in the glass. The shaven head and reduced eyebrows were a definite improvement.

To the left, a few feet along the hall from the Transylvanian leech, stood a glass-fronted cabinet containing a selection of animal skulls, mostly small mammals. Above that was a reproduction of Goya's *Saturn*. Past the door on that side, filling an alcove to the left of the stairs, was a moth-eaten stuffed hyena. Mounted on the facing wall, a fully-articulated crocodile skeleton appeared to be creeping downward at an angle, as if preparing to attack. The crocodile was bookended by a pair of African ritual masks that had given Victor nightmares when he was a child.

The left-hand door led to what Uncle Vortigern liked

to call the library, while that on the right opened on the sitting room. Behind the door by the staircase was the dining room, where another door led to the kitchen. In turn, three more doors led to the back garden, via a conservatory; a large pantry that doubled as a laundry room; and a cellar that Victor had never entered. God alone knew what Uncle Vortigern kept down there.

Upstairs, the house boasted four bedrooms, two bathrooms, and a playroom still filled with toys and games from when Uncle Vortigern and Victor's father Vincent were children – including a doll's house and a rocking horse, and a long shelf lined with ventriloquist dummies. Victor went in there once, when he was six, and refused to enter it ever again.

There was also an attic stacked with sagging tea-chests and cardboard boxes of books, photograph albums, family papers, antique clothing and long-abandoned bric-a-brac. That was another place the young Victor preferred to avoid, if only because of the huge mousetraps hidden in strategic positions. That would need sorting and clearing out. A skip would be needed. A big one. And sturdy gloves.

As he strolled through the ground floor rooms, Victor strove to bring to mind the faces of his spinster great-aunts, the bizarre triplets Veronica, Violet and Victoria, and his wizened grandfather, Vivian Netherwold, the legendary drunkard who had presided over the collapse of the family business. Vauxhall Varieté, set up in 1896 by the shadowy Vitus Netherwold and rumoured to have been bankrolled from the proceeds of a discreet vice operation catering to the exotic fancies of the great and good, supplied a range of goods for the entertainment industry in all its forms –

carnival heads, masks and dummies; stage magicians' props, dancers' costumes and cosmetics; trick cards, sheet music and megaphones; every kind of musical instrument from the autoharp to the zither. You name, and if it had to do with singing, dancing, acting, conjuring or juggling, Vauxhall Varieté made it, sold it, and made a surprising packet out of it. It was said that profits were quietly boosted by old Vitus continuing to provide flagellants, midgets, bearded ladies, dog-faced boys, pinheads, hermaphrodites, and teenaged virgins of all ages and colours, and both sexes, to pique the sexual interests of certain select clients, and that the company shipped hashish, opium, morphine and cocaine around the country alongside its regular products. When the dissolute Vitus died during a cocaine and absinthe binge, falling off the top of Tower Bridge on the stroke of midnight while carnally joined to a Norwegian sailor and a blind East End prostitute known locally as Tuppeny Tess, no one who knew him was surprised. The family couldn't even hush it up – when the bodies were discovered on the bridge, the impact had rammed them so thoroughly and intimately together that they had to be separated *in situ* by a doctor's knife, cheered on by a crowd of around sixty drunken toffs, street walkers, mariners on shore leave, and two nuns who really should have known better. After that, things were taken care of in rather a hurry. Vitus Netherwold may have been buried with a penis, but it wasn't his and it wasn't where it should have been.

Victor smiled as he remembered Vortigern telling him that story. His uncle – tall, handsome and with a full head of hair, as unlike Victor as it was possible to get without belonging to a different race – had chuckled throatily and winked lewdly. It was most inappropriate. Victor had only been ten at the time. And it happened in the churchyard, at his father's funeral, with the vicar and Victor's newly-widowed mother standing next to them.

That funeral had been well-attended. Victor and his mother, his father's friends and colleagues from the factory, Vortigern, a scattering of neighbours, all gathered round the open grave as the coffin was lowered down. Afterward, there had been sandwiches, cakes and sherry at the modest council house Victor had been forced to vacate a decade later when his mother followed her husband into whatever existence, if any, awaited after death. That day, sombre yet celebratory in its way, had been a far cry from the lonely ritual Victor had just attended – excluding the vicar and undertakers, Vortigern was seen off by a meagre gathering consisting only of Victor and his uncle's solicitor, Mr Wainwright, along with three furtive-looking middle-aged men who Victor didn't recognise and who slipped away as soon as the vicar finished his half-hearted speech. Then the solicitor hurriedly muttered his condolences and scuttled off after presenting Victor with an envelope containing a set of keys and an enigmatic letter written in a neat, old-fashioned copperplate script.

Dear Victor,

One has to face facts and the fact is I'm not getting any younger. I reckon I have another year or two left, maybe as many as five, if I'm lucky. It's time to make preparations. You're going to inherit everything. It's quite a lot. I was quite surprised when I totted it all up last night. Your grandfather didn't leave us much when he popped his clogs, the feckless old bastard. As the elder son, I got the house and what remained of his cash, which was a miserable bloody pittance – and those silly old biddies, of course. I inherited responsibility as well as property, you see. Your great-aunts were a pain in the arse but I did my duty and took care of them until they went to the Great Madhouse in the Sky. You probably don't remember but they all died on the same day, within minutes of each other. Fitting for triplets, I suppose. I have no idea which one went first. I never could tell the old bats apart. That was a couple of years before your father died. Luckily, my fortunes were on the up by then, thanks to sound investment advice, or I could never have afforded their funeral. Do you have any idea how much a custom-built three-person coffin costs? I had to do it that way because I didn't want to risk burying them in the wrong graves. They wouldn't have liked that. Besides, they were inseparable in life, so why not in death? But I digress. I've had a damned good life, on the whole. It's been fun and I haven't stinted myself. My only regret is that I didn't do a lot more of everything. That's probably just as well for you, as la bonne vie *doesn't come cheap. Suffice it to say that you are now the proud owner of the house that's been in our family for over a hundred years, along with a considerable amount of money. Like me, you have also inherited responsibility. I wish you the very best of luck. You've always been a good boy and it's such a shame we haven't been able to see much of each other for so many years. I'm sure you'll do the right thing.*

Your loving uncle,
Vortigern Netherwold.

The letter, dated three years previously, affected Victor deeply. His uncle had not been an affectionate man, and this was the closest Vortigern had come to expressing any kind of approval. It also brought back memories of his great-aunts, dressed in voluminous black lace dresses, elbow gloves and mantillas, three tall old ladies wandering side-by-side through the gloomy house like phantoms from a 1930s horror film, conversing quietly in their shared, secret language, occasionally throwing up their hands and shrilly uttering doom-laden prophecies that would never come to pass. Victor thought of their hawk noses, crazed eyes and badly-applied make-up, and shuddered. They had always smelled of mothballs, peppermint and vintage urine. Not once had they acknowledged his existence, and for that he was thankful.

His uncle, Victor decided, had been a nice man. True, he swore like a trooper and wasn't what you'd call sociable, and between noon and bedtime he tended to sway a bit when he walked and smell strongly of whisky; and he had a habit of telling risqué stories to the wrong people at the wrong time. It was also true that he rarely had a good word to say about anyone but Mrs Swinburne, the long-suffering but broadminded Irish lady who cleaned the house and cooked his meals. But he'd never been known to do any actual harm to a single living creature. He'd looked after his insane aunts as best he could, fed the birds, squirrels and foxes that frequented his untidy gardens, and wore a poppy every November. It was a mystery to Victor that a kind, handsome man like Vortigern had never married and had children of his own. Perhaps the old fellow had never found a woman to live up to his own high standards – or even down to his low ones. Then again, Vortigern had already been in his early forties when the three aunts died, and no sane woman would have wanted to share a house with those twittering horrors. Maybe he'd just left it too late.

And now Victor was in the house again, only this time it was his. He smiled to himself, switched off the light, and went back to his little flat to finalise arrangements for his move and phone the print shop to tell his boss he was quitting. He'd said goodbye to Vortigern – now he was saying hello to the future.

Unable to bring himself to take Vortigern's old bedroom, Victor moved his possessions into the only spare room with empty closets. There wasn't much to unpack. A couple of boxes of books and DVDs; his new clothes – so far amounting only to half a dozen shirts, a couple of jackets, two pairs of jeans, some underwear, and a pair of Reebok trainers; a duvet, sheets and pillows; and, of course, his collection of erotic magazines. Other than some toiletries and personal papers, that was all he deemed worth keeping. The rest had been donated to charity shops, recycling bins or landfill.

For an elderly man, Vortigern seemed to have been unusually clued-up on modern technology. The sitting room had a large LCD television set with an internet connection, hooked up to a hard-disc recorder, Blu-ray player and quadrophonic speakers. In the library a matt black PC and monitor as devoid of logos and insignia as any US black ops helicopter sat on a desk of the same hue and finish. Victor's brief survey of the ground floor had also turned up a Nexus 7, a Kindle Fire, two Samsung smartphones and an iPod. Yet while Vortigern was known to watch television regularly – he was fond of soap operas and period dramas – Victor had never known his uncle to use any mobile devices. Indeed, Vortigern had once cheerfully claimed to be unable to programme his old VCR and was constantly complaining about the internet's detrimental effect on social interaction. What was he doing with all this equipment? None of it had been there on Victor's last visit.

The library held other surprises. The latest print copy of *Encyclopaedia Britannica* was perhaps only to be expected, but the shelves included dictionaries in what seemed to be every living human language, along with Latin, Esperanto and Klingon. Software manuals stood alongside books about the stock markets, advanced economics and political theory, history and philosophy, human anatomy and theoretical physics. Most were recent editions. The only material that Victor could relate to Uncle Vortigern were the complete works of A. A. Milne, a dozen or so *Biggles* paperbacks, *My Secret Life*, some spy and crime novels, and two battered old *Beano* annuals. They didn't go so well with the reproductions of Courbet's *L'Origine du monde* and Dalí's *Autumn Cannibalism* on the walls flanking the door, nor with the shrunken heads, voodoo dolls and erotic figurines on the mantelpiece – but, like the ornaments, those older books were at recognisably to Vortigern's taste, which had never strayed too far from the macabre, the childish, or the downright filthy. Even though they were clearly in the majority, the textbooks didn't belong.

At least the kitchen was as Victor remembered it. Everything was as old and worn as it should have been, except for the microwave cooker. Mrs Swinburne, bless her, had cleaned Vortigern's old food from the refrigerator and pantry and replaced it with fresh produce. The only odd note there was the one left pinned to a corkboard by Mrs Swinburne, apologising for the excessive amount of green salad leaves, celery and cucumber, and explaining that Vortigern had on several occasions impressed upon her that this level of greengrocery was to be maintained at all costs, even in the event of his death, and she had no idea why it was so important.

Victor shrugged when he read the note. Another of his uncle's eccentricities, like the stuffed grizzly bear in the sitting room or the voodoo dolls lined up on his dressing table. And the less said about the pine coffin propped up in the utility room, the better; Victor dreaded the prospect of opening *that*. Still, he was getting a good idea of what he could live with and what had to go. The only room left to explore was the cellar, and he expected that, like cellars everywhere, it was full of broken furniture, pots of congealed paint and other stuff he would never find a use for, dust and spiders and mouse droppings. But he still braced himself for shocks when he turned the key and unlocked the door, then groped around until he found the light switch.

It was just as well. The neon tube flickered on to reveal a steep wooden staircase without a handrail. That could have been tricky to negotiate in the dark. Victor descended halfway and surveyed the clean, tidy space. There was no clutter or junk at all, only a small table, a spotless hand basin with a shiny chrome mixer tap, and a single bed. And, sitting on the bed, a hairless, noseless, earless figure with a wide slit for a mouth and bulging black eyes. Its head was shaped like an inverted turnip and its smooth skin was dull grey with a hint of green. There were six fingers on each hand. No more than four feet tall and dressed in a baggy blue coverall, it sat motionless and apparently staring up at the cellar door. At first Victor thought it was another of Vortigern's strange ornaments, some improbable tribal *objet d'art* or an exhibit acquired from a freak show. He nearly filled his trousers when the thing spoke.

'Who the fuck are *you*?' it said in heavily accented English.

Victor's lips opened and closed like an unlatched door in a gale. His knees turned to jelly and began to buckle. His heart raced and his airways seemed to constrict. He wanted to turn and run but his legs refused to move. Instead, he sat heavily on the stair and continued to gape.

The creature's features creased into what might have been a frown. 'Oh, I know. You must be the nephew. Vortigern said you were an ugly bugger.' It eyed Victor critically. 'He wasn't wrong. OK, nephew or whatever your name is, where's Vortigern? I'm bloody starving. Been locked down here for nearly two sodding weeks with only water and three apples to keep me going. I've had to piss and crap in the basin. That took some cleaning, I can tell you.' It stood and approached the stairs. 'Come on, shift your arse. I want some lettuce and cucumber before I forget I can't eat meat and start munching on you.'

In a kind of trance, Victor stood and stepped to one side to allow the creature to ascend. Then he followed it and watched as it opened the fridge, took out half the salad vegetables, and sat at the kitchen table. It stuffed leaves by the handful into that strange mouth, bit off and chewed half a cucumber in one go, and kept on until every last morsel was devoured. When it had eaten its fill, it licked its lips with a forked, reptilian tongue and belched loudly. 'That's the only trouble with this diet. Gas. I'll probably start farting in a few minutes. Anyway, you didn't answer my question. Where's Vortigern?'

Victor replied despite himself. 'He's dead. I'm Victor. Who are you?'

'My name is – ,' the creature emitted a lengthy series of vowels and consonants that sounded like someone with chronic bronchitis and an adenoid problem speaking Dutch backwards through a kazoo. 'But Vortigern calls me Valentine. Called, I suppose I should say. Poor old Vortigern. What a bugger. Still, he was getting on a bit for a human. How did it happen?'

'Heart attack in the betting shop. He'd just won a Yankee. It was the last race that did it. Dead before he hit the floor, so they reckon.'

Valentine nodded. 'Good. At least it was quick and he didn't suffer. And those horses I picked for him came in. He was always rubbish at studying form. So, are you going to look after me now?'

'Me? Look after you? What do you mean?'

The creature sighed impatiently. 'Well, I can't exactly go to Asda looking like this, can I? People would talk. Vortigern did all the household shopping when Mrs Swinburne was on her holidays or when I needed a top-up. You can't really buy fresh salad and that on the internet. They always give you stuff that's right on its bloody sell-by date, the cheap bastards. Limp lettuce and rubbery cucumber. Bloody horrible. Anyway, if Vortigern's dead, you're going to have to do that. He said he was going to leave everything to you. That includes me, sunshine.'

Victor was speechless. He had inherited a – a… 'What are you, exactly?'

Valentine emitted a sound like someone unblocking a sink. Victor realised it was laughing. 'I'm an extraterrestrial, you fuckwit. A being from another world, in a star system far, far away. To be exact, it's the place you lot call Zeta Reticuli. We call it something you'd never be able to pronounce in the time it took you to walk there.'

'How did you get here?'

The creature's eyes shimmered, seemingly its equivalent of rolling them. 'Honestly, how the bloody hell do you think I got here? By bus?'

'Sorry,' said Victor. 'I'm still trying to get my head round this.'

'Understandable, I suppose. And Vortigern said you weren't the sharpest knife in the drawer. Listen, have you ever seen that film? The one where the spaceship flies away and leaves the little fat bloke on Earth? Well, I was that little fat bloke, so to speak. I mean, obviously I'm not fat. Anyway, there I was, wandering around on Clapham Common at one o'clock in the morning wondering what the bleeding hell I was supposed to do – we can't just phone home, you know, and anyway I didn't have the technical skills to build an interocitor or whatever – when up comes Vortigern. Admittedly, he'd had a few drinks. More than a few, if truth be told. But he didn't seem at all surprised to see me. I couldn't understand a word he said but I got the message. He was offering me somewhere to kip for the night. So we got into a car and he drove me here.'

'Hang on – Vortigern didn't have a driving license. He never owned a car.'

'It wasn't exactly his motor, if you know what I mean. He could be impulsive after a few drinks. I helped him hot-wire it. Now stop interrupting. Where was I? When we got here Vortigern went to bed and took me with him. He wanted to, you know, get to know me better. But we weren't compatible. It was a shame, because he wasn't a bad-looking bloke by human standards and I wouldn't have said no. Tell me, Victor – are you married? Girlfriend?'

Victor shook his head, as much to clear it as to indicate the negative. His brain seemed to be fading in and out of the conversation. 'I'm afraid not.'

Valentine seemed disappointed. 'Oh, so you take after your uncle. Never mind. Anyway, that was how it began, back in 1990. I've been very comfortable here, I must say. My own room – I don't usually live in the bloody cellar, Vortigern locks me in there when Mrs Swinburne's due – plenty of food, entertainment… Well, I had quite a bit of time on my hands so I learned to read and speak English, and all your other languages. It wasn't too difficult, really. I'm thinking of learning Akkadian and Sumerian next, and I reckon I can crack Etruscan and Linear A. I was the expedition's exo-linguist, and I was the fucking *best*, if I say so myself. I'm even fluent in Betelgeusian, and they literally talk out of the arses. Gas generated in their digestive tract is forced through anal membranes to create sound, speech. It's best not to stand too close to them when you're having a chat. Would you like to hear a few words?'

'No thanks,' said Victor hastily. 'So that's all you've done since 1990? Learn terrestrial languages?'

'Of course not. I do have other interests, you know. I was really good at maths at school, and I've always been interested in other cultures' economic systems. Your uncle was a bit strapped for cash, so in return for his hospitality I gave him tips on the horses – fascinating sport, we have one just like it at home – and the stock market. We made a pretty penny over the years. It's even easier now you have the internet and mobile phones. Took you lot long enough to come up with them, but what do you expect from a bunch of bloody monkeys? Too busy fighting wars and stitching one another up to get anything constructive done. And reality TV – what's that all about, eh? Who dreams up that crap? Give me a bleeding break. Mind you, I really loved *The Tudors* and *Downton Abbey*. And I'm a huge fan of your old science fiction films. They're so funny. I crack up every time I watch *The Day the Earth Stood Still*. Did Mrs Swinburne lay in any beer? I could do with a pint.'

'You drink beer?'

'Well, of course I drink beer. Beer is one of the standards by which we measure a species' progress, a hallmark of civilisation. It's the universal beverage of choice. Even those spindly buggers from Alpha Centauri have beer, and they use their own excrement as perfume and eat their first-born. But that's no more than you'd expect from overgrown stick insects, I suppose.'

'So we're considered civilised by extraterrestrial standards?'

'Don't fucking push it.' Valentine opened the fridge and extracted four bottles of Bishop's Finger, then opened two with an implement that appeared to be built into its coverall. 'Here, get your laughing gear round this.'

Victor struggled to take it all in. While he could, on an intellectual level, accept the existence of life on other worlds, actually talking to an alien — and drinking beer with it — was something else entirely. The fact that his late uncle had befriended and sheltered this unearthly being somehow only made it more difficult to come to terms with. At least the creature's speech patterns were now explicable. It spoke just like Uncle Vortigern and was equally foul-mouthed.

'Do your people swear in your own language?'

'Of course we fucking do. That's another measure of civilisation, making reference to excretory and sexual functions and physiology to express disdain, emphasise parts of speech, and make jokes. Our psychologists reckon it's how we distance ourselves from our origins as lower animals. They say it's the sociobiological equivalent of buying a bigger house or faster car to show you are better than your neighbours. It's all bollocks. I mean, it's not as if we've stopped getting rid of our bodily wastes or having sex, is it? Far from it. A good sewage system is a hallmark of civilisation. And the more highly evolved a species becomes, the more it thinks about sex, and the more sex it has. Look at you lot — bloody obsessed with it. You invent the internet, the most advanced and sophisticated method of communication and information dispersal in your history, and what do you use it for? Sharing films and photos of people shagging, that's what. That and cat videos. I like those. Anyway, I'm not saying there's anything wrong with that. We're the same as you in that respect. Everyone is. Not the cat videos, though. We have something called the — well, let's not go there. More beer?'

Four hours later, slightly drunk, his head bursting with information he was unable to adequately process, and slightly alarmed at Valentine's behaviour after a few beers, Victor went for a lie down in his chosen bedroom, leaving the extraterrestrial contentedly nibbling rocket and Chinese leaves while it surfed the internet, catching up on the news and checking that Uncle Vortigern's investments – now Victor's, of course – were still giving satisfactory returns.

So, he thought, Vortigern had been sheltering an alien racing tipster and financial advisor for twenty-five years. That explained a lot – the sudden restrictions his uncle had placed on visits not long after Victor's fourteenth birthday, the healthy bank balance and other assets, the secretiveness. Anyone else would have announced the visitor to the world – YouTube, Facebook, the tabloids. Vortigern could have made a fortune without needing to play the stock market. But that would have meant the authorities taking a close interest in his uncle's affairs, and Vortigern hated the authorities. He would have baulked at the idea of government scientists, intelligence agents, the military and God knows who else crawling all over his property. And Valentine would have ended up in some secret lab being tested, interrogated, and probably sliced thinly for microscope slides.

An alien. An intelligent non-human from another planet. Victor had been talking to an alien. And having a beer with it. Chatting away at the kitchen table as if it was the most normal thing in the world. Well perhaps in some worlds it was. Perhaps in some worlds it was normal to…

The thought faded and vanished away before it crystallised. Victor slept.

When he awoke, the first thing he saw was Valentine standing by the bed, staring at him and gnawing thoughtfully on a stick of celery. The alien lifted a leg and emitted a lengthy, impressively loud and oddly musical fart. The stench was appalling.

'Bloody hell,' said Victor, his face creasing in disgust. 'That is seriously vile. You might have done that outside.'

'I was saying "good morning" in Betelgeusian,' replied Valentine. 'Sorry about the methane and hydrogen sulphide by-products – unavoidable, I'm afraid.'

Victor scowled and tried to waft the smell away with a pillow. The effort was wasted because Valentine farted again.

'What did that one mean?'

'Oh, that was just a fart. It's the herbivore diet, you know. My people don't even notice it.'

'Well, my people do, so please try to hold it in. Anyway, what are you doing in here? Don't I get any privacy?'

'I didn't think you'd mind. Vortigern didn't. Do you have a car?'

'Yes,' replied Victor. 'That's how I got my stuff here. Why?'

'In that case, I wonder if you'd mind taking me out for a drive. I can wear a hooded top and sunglasses. No one will notice me.'

Of course, thought Victor. The alien had been effectively a prisoner in Vortigern's house for a quarter of a century. He felt a sudden pang of sympathy for Valentine – abandoned, stranded far from home, alone, confined to quarters. 'It must be terrible for you, being cooped up here all the time.'

'Oh, it's not so bad. Back home we don't go out much. Our society is very home-centred. Besides, I often stroll in the gardens at night, and in summer when the trees and bushes are in full leaf and the neighbours can't see into the garden I go out in the daytime. It's nice to get a bit of fresh air and see the local wildlife. I'm not too keen on those little buggers with the fluffy tails since one of them chased me on Clapham Common that night, but the birds remind me of home.'

'You have birds on your world?'

'Not exactly, but they're close enough if you squint a bit. They sing like your birds, especially when the sun's going down. It's very romantic. Always puts me in the mood. It's a pity you're so like your uncle.'

'Eh?'

'You know, gay. Don't worry, there's nothing to be ashamed of. We have gays, too. That's one of the hallmarks of civilisation — our psychologists reckon it's to do with liberating sexual desire from the reproductive urge. Personally, I think that's bollocks, too. I think you just fancy what you fancy and that's all there is to it. I mean, you can't really evolve to not reproduce, can you? That would be as far as you could go. It stands to reason.'

Victor reddened. 'Uncle Vortigern wasn't gay. And I'm definitely not.'

'Oh, really?' Valentine laughed again. 'So what do you think he was doing on Clapham Common at one in the morning? Why do you think a wealthy bloke like him, handsome in human terms, never had a girlfriend or a wife? Look in his address book — nearly all men, apart from his

GP and Mrs Swinburne. You'll also find the phone numbers of several gay clubs and bars. As I said, Victor, there's no need to be ashamed. It doesn't bother me one little bit. It's perfectly normal, and it's legal here, just like it is back home. Not my cup of tea, but there you go.'

'But I'm not – Vortigern was *gay*? Blimey. I had no idea.'

'He was as gay as a night out in *fin de siècle* Paris. Old school gay, very discreet, but absolutely gay. That's why we were incompatible. He was so gay he didn't even fancy a hot babe like me.'

'A hot babe like – wait a minute. You're *female*?'

The eyes shimmered. 'Shit, you really are a bit slow. Of course I'm female.'

'You mean female in the same sense as a human female is female?'

'God, you really are fucking thick, Victor Netherwold. Yes, I have pretty much the same genitalia as a human female, just as human males have something very similar to males of my species, though from what I've seen on your internet porn sites I'd say the human ones are smaller on average. Sexual reproduction is the only way to ensure sufficient genetic variation for intelligent beings to evolve. That means a minimum of two sexes. In fact, we've never encountered intelligent life that has more than two sexes, though there are a couple of hermaphroditic species that have developed culture and technology nearly equivalent to yours and mine. Nature tends to be economical. The sexual apparatus is fairly constant, though. If you think about it, it's the most efficient arrangement. And in higher species the female chooses her mate according to what she considers desirable characteristics, including intelligence, temperament, physique and mating technique. Sexual selection, in evolutionary terms. It's the same everywhere. It's another – '

'– hallmark of civilisation. Yeah, I get the picture. Bloody Nora.'

Valentine was quiet as they drove more or less aimlessly through South West London. Victor dutifully pointed out what he considered the architectural and cultural highlights – the Oval cricket ground, the MI6 building at the southern end of Vauxhall Bridge, Battersea Power Station – but the little alien seemed uninterested. When they reached Kew, Victor stopped the car and asked what was wrong.

'I'm bored.' She gestured at the high wall surrounding the Royal Botanical Gardens. 'OK, it's nice to see the place in daylight, but it's not the same as actually *seeing* it. You know, walking around, experiencing it properly. And these bloody sunglasses keep sliding off. I don't have those things you have that hold them up.'

'Ears and a nose,' said Victor helpfully.

'Yeah, I don't have those. And I'm hot and thirsty. I want a beer.'

'You can have a beer when we get home.'

Valentine folded her arms and pouted as well as she was able with that strange mouth. 'I want one *now*,' she said. 'And I'm hungry.'

'Tell you what,' Victor sighed. 'We passed a corner shop a mile or two down the road. We'll go back and I'll see what I can find. Just don't get out of the car, OK?'

Valentine gave him her species' equivalent of a glare.

'I'm not bloody stupid, Victor Netherwold. I'm the ultimate illegal immigrant. If I get caught they'll put me in that horrible Yarl's Wood place. UKIP will go barmy. Well, barmier.'

'I think UKIP and Yarl's Wood might be the least of your worries. Joe at work reckons there's a top secret research facility under Mornington Crescent tube station where the government keeps all its recovered alien technology and, you know, specimens. You'd probably end up being experimented on, maybe even dissected.'

'What, like you lot reckon we do to you? Rectal probes and all that Whitley Streiber stuff? Do me a favour. That's not what civilised species get up to. Well, except for the Aldebaran lot. But they regard anything without tentacles and an exoskeleton as fair game. We try to avoid them. They're always conducting so-called tests wherever they land. Between you and me, I think they're just a bunch of perverts. They have these big, barbed organic tech things they put up your – '

'Oh, look – there's a man walking a ferret on a lead,' Victor interjected, pointing vaguely into the distance. 'That's something you don't see every day.' While his passenger was distractedly looking for the fictitious mustelid and its escort, Victor parked and applied the handbrake, then cracked open the door. 'Any particular brew you fancy? How about a bottle of wine or something?'

'I can't drink wine or spirits – they bring me out in a bright yellow rash. And cider makes my shoulders ache. Any decent beer will do. Ruddles or Adnams, anything like that. While you're there you may as well stock up for tonight. There's only one bottle of Bishop's Finger left in the fridge. Get a couple of dozen.'

'A couple of dozen? Don't you think you might have a bit of a problem?'

Valentine blinked slowly. 'What do you mean?'

'I mean a drink problem,' said Victor, leaning into the car. 'You drank most of the beer Mrs Swinburne left in the fridge, and those two crates you found in the larder. Now all you're going on about is beer. I know what that suggests to me.'

The alien sighed. 'Don't be so bloody silly. It isn't like *The Man Who Fell to Earth*, you know. I'm not bloody Thomas Jerome Newton, sitting around getting arseholed on gin to ease the pain of being alone and waiting for his planet to die. My people are made of stronger stuff than that. Besides, most species metabolise beer in a completely different way from you humans. It doesn't affect us the same way. We can hold our beer. We don't get drunk.'

Victor raised an eyebrow. 'So last night when you put a pair of Vortigern's old Y-fronts on your head and started singing in – what was it, Serbo-Croat? Hungarian? – that had nothing to do with the beer?'

'I was just letting off steam,' said Valentine sulkily. 'What do you want me to do, drown in existential angst? And that song was "Girls Just Want to Have Fun" in Navajo. I translated it myself.'

Silently, Victor thanked his lucky stars that she hadn't treated him to 'Like a Virgin' in Armenian, or given a rendition of 'I Kissed a Girl' in Swahili. Or any Lady Gaga song in English.

The headache was bad. The taste in his mouth was worse.

Opening his eyes to the morning sun was a torment. And turning gingerly onto his side and seeing the back of Valentine's head on the other pillow – well, that was simply heart-stopping.

Victor gaped. He gasped. He blinked. He closed his eyes tightly for a full minute and hoped it was only a dream. When he opened them again, the pain in his head told him he was definitely awake. And she was still there. Experimentally, he felt beneath the duvet. He touched bare, warm flesh, smooth and silky. As he ran his hand along her side, Valentine purred in her sleep. Across the room, the blue coverall was draped over a chair. Carefully, Victor returned to a supine position and closed his eyes once more.

Fragmented memories of the previous evening returned. He remembered snatches of conversation, Valentine singing 'Big Yellow Taxi' in Japanese. He recalled drinking rather more beer than he was used to. Then trying to convince Valentine that he wasn't gay. Then her eventual response. *Prove it.*

And he had. He'd been pleasantly surprised by the sight of her shapely, if breastless, naked body. She had a nice bum. Moonlight and sexual arousal made her features seem oddly human – though the beer was undoubtedly a factor there. Although the experience was a bit of a blur, he'd certainly enjoyed it. Her skin was as warm and vibrant as he'd imagined any woman's would be. That forked tongue had been exciting; and, as she'd said, her sexual apparatus was pretty much identical to those Victor had seen in his porn mags, and seemed to work in exactly the same way. It had been good – very good indeed.

Victor shook his head, grimacing at the sharp pain that followed. He'd finally lost his virginity. And how many men could honestly say they'd popped their cherry with a female alien? He put his hands behind his head and smiled widely. There were probably ethical considerations. But as far as Victor knew, the laws against sex with non-human species only applied to terrestrial animals. She'd been on earth for over twenty years, so Valentine was certainly not under-age. Their coupling had been by mutual, if drunken, consent. It might have been irregular but there was no way it was illegal.

He dozed. When he awoke again, the hangover was less severe. Valentine was looking at him, her eyes squeezed slightly shut like an affectionate cat. He was learning her body-language.

'I lied about the beer not affecting me,' she said. 'Though I do metabolise it differently, so I don't have a hangover. Well, not much of one.' Victor realised she was still purring. She stroked his chest. 'Well, neither of us is a virgin anymore.'

Victor was astonished. 'You mean you hadn't either? Last night you seemed so, well – experienced, uninhibited.'

'I could say the same about you. Instinct, Victor. My people, like yours, worry about the social consequences and that usually gets in the way until they know each other well. The beer loosened us up, instinct took over, good old unbridled lust did the rest. It worked for me. And I must say you seemed to be enjoying yourself.'

'Blimey.'

'You know, for a human you're relatively presentable. I could have done much worse on my home world.

Technically, I was only a girl when I arrived on Earth, only around thirty of your years – too young to be pair-bonded, sexually immature. Stuck here, I thought I'd never get my leg over. I had no idea what it would be like to actually do it, only what I'd seen on a screen. But it was different from the porn videos on my world or yours. I wasn't expecting, I don't know – that tenderness, intimacy, the emotional connection. It was even better than I thought it would be. Shame about those things that stick out of the side of your head, though.'

'That would be my ears. Bloody hell. What do we do now?'

A six-fingered hand slid down to Victor's groin and gently massaged what it found there, which stirred interestedly.

'We could do it again,' Valentine suggested.

'Well, that was a surprise.'

Valentine had just returned from the bathroom, to which she'd rushed as soon as they returned from their trip to the Bluewater shopping centre. They'd been out in public together a couple of dozen times now, with Valentine wearing the blue *burqa* Victor had ordered online – an idea he'd got from watching a television documentary about Afghanistan – and he'd discovered she was as fond of shopping as any human woman of his admittedly limited experience. She complained that the *burqa* was too hot, that it made her itch, and that it was undignified; but she was evidently pleased to be able to get out and about to do relatively normal things without people thinking her any more of a curiosity than the average strict Muslim woman in London and the Home Counties. Sometimes they went to boroughs with large Asian or African populations – usually Newham, Brent or Tower Hamlets – and she would converse with shopkeepers and their families in Tamil, Hindi or Urdu, Amharic or Arabic. If any were shocked or surprised by the large amounts of beer she bought, they didn't show it.

They were, Victor understood, beginning to live like a normal couple. They slept together, had regular and mutually satisfying sex, discussed the morning news over breakfast, watched television, went out to concerts and the cinema, and took long walks in various parks, always hand in hand, and always with Valentine wearing the *burqa*. True, they had the occasional argument. But wasn't that part of any relationship? Victor was happy. He hoped Valentine was happy too. That was important to him. She was important to him.

Now she held something wrapped in the folded *burqa*, which she hadn't had time to remove before hurrying to the loo. 'I thought I just had an upset stomach,' she said. 'It felt like I needed an urgent camel's. I wasn't expecting this. To be honest, I didn't think it was possible.'

Victor was intrigued. 'What is it?'

With a flourish, Valentine unveiled a shiny emerald green egg, about ten inches from top to bottom. She gazed at Victor with those feline, hooded eyes in the way that signified affection and contentment.

Victor's jaw dropped. 'Blimey, is that what I think it is? I thought you'd put on a bit of weight lately but I didn't like to say. Men here tend not to say that to their partners. Human women are touchy about that sort of thing. Is it –

you know – *viable*?'

She beamed. 'Yes, it is. I can hear him purring inside the shell. Victor, this is your son.'

'A son? How do you know it's a boy?'

'Males always come in green eggs, females in blue. Something to do with the hormone balance affecting pigmentation. Green for a boy, blue for a girl, as our saying goes, more or less. That's why I was wearing a blue coverall. We're sticklers for tradition. It's why I insisted on a blue *burqa*.'

'It's a nice shade of green,' Victor observed, unable to think of anything else to say.

'It's not the usual shade. That's probably because he's half-human. Normally they're darker, more olive. His shell is gorgeous, so bright.'

'Do you have to sit on it?'

'I'm not a bloody ostrich,' she replied crossly. 'When your birds lay eggs, they are just fertilised ova. With my people the eggs are laid when the embryonic stage has passed and the children are already well-developed foetuses, nourished by a substance that's a cross between a placenta and an egg white. We hatch them about a week after they're laid. They can't break out on their own so we'll have to do it for him. Traditionally, the parents do it together. I'll know when he's ready by the noises he makes.'

'What sort of noises?'

'Hungry noises. Here, hold him. And speak to him. You have to speak to them so they know you when they hatch. And give him a name so he'll know who he is. That's what my people do.'

Reverently, with greater care than he'd ever taken with

anything in his life, Victor took the egg from Valentine's outstretched hands and cradled it in his arms. This was momentous – the first alien-human hybrid child on Earth, as far as he knew. More importantly, it was his son. He wondered what the boy would look like. He wondered how he would get the birth registered so the kid could go to school, obtain a national insurance number, have prospects. That, he decided, was something to worry about in the years to come. They had plenty of money and with Valentine's financial wizardry he was sure they'd soon have plenty more, the kind of wealth that made anything possible. Money can't buy happiness but it can get things done. Happiness had arisen in the most unlikely way, from an inheritance he hadn't anticipated. Now it was time to ensure that inheritance was only the present phase of a lasting heritage. The weight of this new responsibility felt good.

He held the egg close to his face and spoke against the shell, feeling the new life within moving in response to his voice. 'Vivian, my boy – one day all this will be yours.'

About the Author

Alby Stone was born and raised in Southend-on-Sea in Essex and now lives and works in London. He has written several novels and a number of short stories.

http://vaingloriouslunacy.com
http://clerkenwellwritersasylum.wordpress.com/

More fiction by Alby Stone

The Forgotten Stars
Secret Songs
The Hand of Fire
(The *Havensea* trilogy)

The Sorrows of Angels
The Shadow Woman
Disappearer
Intruder
The Gorgon's Daughters
(The *Wonderland Investigations* series)

A Yellow Room
(A prequel to the *Havensea* and *Wonderland Investigations* books)

Cherry Blood
Dummy
A Single Drop of Night
The Girl in the Tie-Dye Dress
Fox
Woodwise

Sparks and Ashes: Short Fiction

Printed in Great Britain
by Amazon